C000151739

Out of the ruins

Out of the

Out of the ruins

Roger Wheatley

Out of the ruins Copyright © by Roger Wheatley. All Rights Reserved.

The author lives in Australia's capital city, Canberra, with his wife, two sons, a dog and a cat.

This is his second novel. The first, *Wolves in white collars,* is available on Kindle.

outoftheruinsbook@gmail.com

Thanks to my ever-patient wife for her love and encouragement.

Prologue

There was no moon, plenty of stars but no moon. A can't-see-my-hand-in-front-of-my-face kind of darkness. I saw the headlights long before I heard the vehicle, just a glimpse, a snatch of searing light through the branches of the scrappy Greek-island scrub. But then it was gone. The only sound—which at first I thought was my tinnitus—was the water softly buffeting the coarse sand of the cove somewhere not far to our right.

"Here they come," I whispered. It was a pretty stupid thing to say. Of course it was them, who else was going to be bouncing along a rutted, isolated track on a Greek island at this time of night. But fear will do that to you.

We probably should have separated to be more effective, we both had guns. I'm sure if I'd suggested it Anna would have been up for it. She was brave, and competent. I was neither. And given my shooting experience amounted to missing slow-moving ducks with a BB gun in side-show alley, I figured it best not to suggest it. So we stayed where we were, tucked in behind our log.

I nearly soiled myself when the man walked past a few minutes later. He was a wraith. He'd come from nowhere and obviously done this kind of work before. We shouldn't be here. He was almost close enough to touch. I could smell his body odour. He needed a shower. He made no sound but it was like I could feel the disturbed air in his wake. He was gone as quickly as he'd appeared. But he hadn't seen us. Then someone whistled, gently, probably him, somewhere off to our right. And then the car was there, no headlights or brake lights, just the softest of sounds as the tyres rolled over the grass of the clearing. I was peeking around one end of the log, Anna the other. A couple of doors clicked open, but no inside light came on. I could see the faint outline of a tall man.

"No trouble from you, big fella." It was an Australian accent. I was a bit stunned. "And you'll likely survive this."

They had Stavros. Shit. I doubted that Stavros would understand what he meant. His English wasn't great. And I doubted whether it mattered. Surely they wouldn't be leaving witnesses.

The car started and then turned and backed up to the edge of the clearing above the sand. This time there were brake lights and I could see three of them, plus Stavros. One climbed down to the beach and another began dropping packages over the edge.

"Gently boys," said the Australian. "We don't want to be trying to sift this shit out of the sand." One of the helpers laughed.

When they'd finished, the bag dropper climbed down to the beach, leaving the Australian alone with Stavros.

I'd barely had time to turn to look at Anna for some inspiration, when a low rumble snapped my head around. For a second I thought there might have been a storm coming. But then realised it was the sound of a powerful engine. It was coming from the right. It had to be a boat. Great, more criminals. Our options were quickly diminishing, and given they had started close to zero, it wasn't looking good.

And then a spotlight swung across the clearing, like the war club of a Norse god through the black. The light settled on Stavros and the

Australian. Both men threw up an arm in perfect sync shielding their eyes. For a moment they looked like they were going to salute.

Stavros must have decided he wouldn't get a better opportunity. He took one step and gave the Australian a shove, and then turned and lumbered for the scrub. The Australian stumbled several paces, barely stopping himself from going over the edge. He raised his gun.

"Run Stavros, run." I couldn't help myself. And then it all went to shit.

Shots cracked from the boat and from the Australian, kicking up sand and wood-chips, bullets thudding into our log. I prayed for stout Greek wood. The spotlight had swivelled towards us. The area around us lit up like day, but we thankfully were hidden in the shadow. The gunfire from the boat ceased. The noise was awful. It had to be some sort of automatic thing, that gun. The racket bounced around the cove for seconds after the firing had stopped.

"Can you see the big fella?" The Australian had moved, probably behind the car.

The spotlight swung away from us and I risked a look. There was no sign of Stavros. I'd probably saved his life. But we were fucked.

1

How the mighty had fallen. A cliche, I know, I'm a writer. I know cliches, been using them for years. Well, had been using them. Using them would imply that I was still writing, and that was technically incorrect. Was I even still a writer? Are you a writer if you're not writing?

Anyway, the longest thing I'd written lately was a handful of spiteful emails to my literary agent. But even that had stopped. There wasn't a lot of point. It wasn't her fault. I was just angry. And scared.

The dream was over. I finally had to admit it. The fame was gone, and with it the largesse of fancy friends, the lifestyle, the advances. A few royalty payments trickled in from time to time, barely enough to keep the wolves from the door, keep the electricity on. I'd spent the advance for the next book, a book that existed only in the existential sense. The publisher had long ago given up hope of seeing a draft. My agent about as confident as the publisher.

I had my apartment in the city, but that was about it.

It was the ideas that had been first to go. Ideas had never been a problem. The publisher knew that, and that's why a few vague words had been enough. They knew I was good for it. Panic didn't set it in straight away. I figured something would come. It always had. But it didn't. Things got started right enough. But it was like peeing in the desert. A big, strong stream, disappearing into nothing. No evidence that there'd ever been anything.

Still, no cause for panic. Even the greats had blocks. But my mojo had vanished like Australia's Lake Eyre. One day there, the next day, gone. No explanation. Just an empty, crusty expanse of hot, dry nothing. And it didn't take long for the vultures to circle. It started with relaxed meetings at the agency. Gentle nudges and references to deadlines but laughed off with a we-know-you'll-come-through-for-us nods to wind up proceedings.

None of it helped. I was like a middle-aged man with performance anxiety. If they were trying to get it up for me, they were going about it the wrong way. The more they talked, the more I shrivelled. I'd never known pressure. It was that reviewer from the daily who started it, asking when the next one was coming, sniffing a problem. And then came others. At first it was the pleading of the faithful, wanting another instalment. It was complimentary. But it didn't take long for the predators to circle.

I didn't know what was worse. A blank screen or a page of drivel, sitting there mocking me, reminding me that I was washed up. The agent told me not to delete the stuff I'd written. Send it to her, she said, we can work together, it can't be as bad as you think. So I sent it. She eventually suggested I stop.

I think the worst of it was that the phone stopped ringing. No-one wanted a long lunch any more, picking up the tab at a fancy eatery for a few hours with the champ. Sad, that's what I was. What a schmuck. I wasn't stupid enough to believe, in the good times, that these people were my friends. It didn't really matter. I was happy enough to have the sycophants and clingers-on. As long as there was a critical mass, enough to create the illusion of good friends sharing good times, that'd been enough.

And then she'd walked out. That hurt a bit, but maybe not enough. And that probably explained why she went. That I didn't care enough. I was still doin' okay at that stage. It was after the last book but I had no reason to believe that there wouldn't be another one. That scenario had been a ways off. So I didn't chase her too hard. Yeah, I asked her to come back a couple of times but I seemed to be going through the motions. She could tell.

She'd put up with a lot. Sitting here now and looking back that was probably the stupidest thing I did—and I did a lot of stupid shit, trust me—that I let her go. I reckon she might have stayed if I'd made the slightest effort. I actually think she liked me, beyond the books, and the money. But, as my old man used to say, that's another ship that's sailed.

I wonder what she'd say if she could see me now, sitting on a bus. Probably nothing. She'd be one of the few who wouldn't laugh at me. There'd be plenty that would. But here I was, sitting on an interstate bus heading off to the international airport. Me, a bunch of Asian students, and a tattooed mother having a tough time with a coughing baby.

This is what it had come to. It used to be a uniformed man in a smart, shiny new sedan, waiting in the driveway. *Yes sir, no sir, love your books sir,* that kind of stuff. Met at the airport, whizzed through the formalities, up the front of the plane. I sat in 3B on the bus, just for the irony, I used to demand it on my international flights. The irony didn't feel good. But this was my last shot, that's how I saw it.

It was a travel story I'd stumbled on, looking at the Internet when I should have been writing. It talked of spring in the Greek islands. Quiet, great weather and—best of all—cheap. A change of scene. It was the drain cleaner I needed to remove the hair-ball from my creative s-bend.

I had enough in the account for a return economy flight to Athens, a cheap hotel and a bit of pocket money. The journey to the airport passed quietly enough. The baby had finally fallen asleep and the whiff of toilet chemicals was not enough to keep me from slumber (a belt or two of Stoli at home, prior to departure had helped).

The international departure area was like a new world for me without a minder from the agency. I gave a nostalgic look towards the business class line and the deferential way they were treated. I had plenty of time to admire it, as I zigged and zagged my way with the great unwashed towards a distant counter with its sneering attendants. Crying children, piles of mismatched luggage, people in tracksuit pants, oh how the mighty had fallen.

"Sir," delivered with all the warmth and sincerity of a prison guard, "all the window seats are gone. As are all the aisle seats. Most people checked-in on line. I'd suggest, in future, that if you have a strong seating preference you do the same."

Too depressed to retort I moved on through the border processes, expecting a gloved hand to top off my day. Perhaps it might have cheered me.

I watched as the well-healed and important took the anonymous elevator ride to the clouds, a world of good food, free alcohol, clean toilets and deferential servants. I moved quickly away. The smell of a thousand perfume samples in the duty free shop threatened to explode my head. I looked across to the shelf of twenty-five year old single-malts. I could taste the smoky, peaty sublimity. But I would have to survive on memories, there'd be no shopping there.

I found a quiet corner in a bar near my boarding gate, sucking down gin and tonics, eating through my meagre pile of cash.

By the time I heard my name over the loudspeaker I was feeling somewhat better. I was mellow enough to completely ignore the filthy look I got at the boarding gate. I don't know if it was habit or hope that made me attempt to turn left as I entered the plane. I was quickly put to rights by the door attendant, with a look that said, 'friend, who are you kidding'. I wanted to scream out, *but that's where I belong. It's all a mistake, I'm important, I want my champagne and hot towel before take-off.*

Passengers stared as I stumbled down the aisle. I needed to pee but was ushered to my seat by an impatient staff member. There was no room in the overhead locker for my bag, so it was carted off into the distance, no doubt being heaved out the back door, such was the treatment here in steerage.

An old man, in his blue, cable-knit jumper, grey tracksuit pants and hearing aid, smiled from the aisle seat, as I gesticulated towards the empty centre spot. His initial attempt to rise came to an abrupt halt when he reached the limit of his loosely adjusted seat belt. He catapulted back into his seat, giving me another smile as he unclasped the offending device. Then, as he rose a second time, he managed to spill his headset, blanket, menu and ablution kit onto the floor.

About thirty minutes later I was in my seat. And I needed to pee, really rather urgently.

By the time the seat belt light went off I was frightened to stand, the pressure of my seatbelt the only thing keeping my bladder in check. The old man didn't look pleased when I implored him to move again. I'm pretty sure he'd only just managed how to figure out where the on-switch was for the in-flight entertainment. While he remembered to undo the seat belt, he managed to tangle himself in his headphone cord, attempting to rise without unplugging it. And once again he dropped his blanket, menu and ablution kit onto the floor.

By the time I got out there was a queue at the toilet. I joined the rabble and clenched, waited, and then finally found relief.

And then I had to get back into my seat. And guess what, my aisle-seat-octagenarian was out to it, or possibly dead. Not sure which was preferable. Dead would be a better long-term prospect, but decidedly inconvenient at this point. He snorted and his eyes shot open like window blinds when I rattled his shoulder. You'd think by now he might have shaved a few tenths off his record for getting out of his seat, or at least improved his technique, dropping less stuff. But no.

I looked towards the guy in the window seat before I entered. The look suggesting, *you might want to take this opportunity, you may not get another.* But he stayed put.

While I climbed in, the old man hobbled off to the bathroom. I was tempted, for his well-being, to hide his headphones, to save him a lot of angst. As I settled I pushed the call button. Alcohol would be required before this was over.

2

I stumbled my way through the Athens arrivals hall. I hadn't had a drink for a few hours—I stopped when they wanted to start charging—so was relatively sober, but feeling rough. With nothing but my carry-on luggage I passed through the welcome festivities quickly, and found myself furiously scrabbling through my bag to find my Ray Bans to ameliorate the effects of Greek sunshine, which was searing my eyeballs like a Bond-film laser.

I found the bus that would take me to Piraeus—the port in Athens—to get my ferry. I caught a brief glimpse of the Acropolis in the distance on the drive. The port was mayhem. There were gates, jetties and ferries in all directions. I stumbled around for ten minutes, fighting off a swarm of kids with a swinging back-pack, and found the ticket window, where a warm welcome was unforthcoming. The woman grunted, handed me my boarding pass, "wharf nine, small ferry. You go."

The ferry ride was pleasant enough. The coffee was decent, I just had to give up a kidney to afford one. I woke from a dribbling slumber as we slowed to enter the small harbour of my Greek island destination. My eyes opened to the sight of four other eyeballs staring at me from the row in front. A sneer sent the cheeky little buggers running to catch their mother.

It was the middle of the day when I stepped onto the jetty and took my first look around.

My first thought was how bloody dry it was. The countryside was all steep peaks and stunted scrub. I could almost feel the the heat radiating from the rocks. A band of white buildings, like dried-out bones, bleached white in the baking sun, clung gamely to the thin strip of flat land between the hills and the sea.

It should have been beautiful. It probably was. But with a day of little sleep and too much booze under my belt all I seemed to notice was how dry my mouth was, how much my eyeballs felt like they'd been rolled across the Sahara, and how the sun was sucking any final remnants of moisture from me.

I needed a beer.

I had a vague recollection that the hotel wasn't far away. Nothing was far away. But gone were the days when someone would be waiting with a printed card in a smart outfit to whisk me off. I dragged my recalcitrant suitcase along the cracked concrete of the landing jetty. Each clack of the wheels sending a surge of the pain through my head.

I'd actually managed to book my own accommodation—no one else was going to do it—but I couldn't remember the name of the place. Something to do with water and Greece.

"Great," I said out loud as I stood in front of a string of water-front hotels: The *Aegean*, the *Mediterranean*, and the *Cycladaen*. I thought it was the first but given I'd paid a deposit, thought I should check, and spent ten minutes looking for some evidence in my bag. It turned out that it was the *Cycladaen*. And if I was in any doubt as to whether I was in the right place, I was put to rights the second I stepped into the foyer.

"Mr Terry, Mr Terry, welcome to my humble hotel. I have been waiting."

She ran to me, balked, and then I could see her throwing away any idea of hotel diplomacy, grabbing me in a vast bear hug. It was not what I needed right now, an adoring fan. Especially when the cloying odour of her hair-spray and perfume permeated every part of my being. I swallowed the small amount of sick in my mouth. It was a close-run thing.

Eventually she stepped back, regaining her composure, smoothing her floral kaftan, enabling me to take a breath of fresh air. She was a big-bosomed woman with big hair, all coiled and balanced on top like she was returning with the day's water from the well.

She insisted on carrying my bag up to the room. She talked the whole way up about my books and how she connected with the characters and what they said to her. I wouldn't have minded the attention, particularly with the dearth of it lately, but I was not at my best. I dreaded trying to get her out of my room. I finally managed to corral her and move her towards the door, locking it securely when she was out. A light tap followed. I opened it, on the safety chain.

"Let me me know if I can do anything for you," were her parting words.

I collapsed onto the bed and took in my surroundings. Well, it wasn't the the Peninsular in Hong Kong, or the Ritz in New York. But it was clean and had a desk and a window looking over the harbour. Spartan but functional. It was like Mickey's gym in the first *Rocky* movie. I took a moment to enjoy the parallel. Yep, just like Rocky. Not expected to win. A chump. It was what I needed.

But I would start fresh tomorrow. No point trying to pump something out when I was tired and smelly. A shower, a walk, some lunch and a nap. That was what I needed. And then I would be ready to make the magic happen, tomorrow.

The shower worked wonders. The water was hot. I even shaved. I dressed in clean clothes and left my room, after a furtive glance to check that Aphrodite—the Greek goddess of love—was not lurking. Thankfully the stairs led to a front door and did not pass through the reception area, so I was able to depart surreptitiously.

This was more like it. I felt tired, but I felt good. I was away from all the things that I knew, things that reminded me of my problems, things that mocked me. And, more importantly, away from the people who knew me best. Here was my chance.

This deserved a celebration.

On a second viewing, I decided the village really was rather splendid. It bent itself around the tiny harbour where colourful fishing dories jigged merrily against their mooring lines. A couple of old men sat on the jetty talking and mending fishing nets. They acknowledged me with a brief head-nod as I passed. A gaggle of local urchins took turns, jumping from the top of a pylon into the clear waters of the harbour.

Further along, a small beach took care of the needs of the few family groups of tourists on the island this early in the season. There were no vast rows of deck chairs and gaudy umbrellas, or beach touts, or hair plaiters. It was whatever the seaside-version of bucolic is.

Half-way up one of the towering peaks, that looked imperiously down over the village, was a ruin of some sort with a rough-looking track wending its way up through the briars, brambles and rocks. It was inspiring. I could feel the words building. For the first time in a long time I felt excited at the prospect of sitting down at my laptop.

I turned back towards my hotel and the harbour where I had spied a couple of tavernas. A woman welcomed me warmly to her almost-empty dining area. It was perfect. I took a table near the edge, the water lapping gently near my feet. She brought me bread and dip and I asked for a Greek beer, while I perused the menu.

A beer had never tasted much better. It was cold, crisp and cleansing, moisture beading on the outside of the bottle. I drained it in short shrift. I ordered meatballs in red sauce—a local specialty the menu informed me—and a simple salad of fetta, cucumber, tomato, onion and olives, doused in olive oil. And I had a small carafe of white wine to wash it all down. It was simplicity itself. I felt a warm rush of humanity to all who came near.

I smiled at everyone who entered the taverna. I even had time for the herd of cats that seemed to take an interest in my presence. This was life. Perhaps this was what Thoreau meant by living deliberately, and fronting only the essential facts of life. But then, even in my state of euphoria, I still thought Thoreau was a bit of a tosser.

I finished off with some halva and a cup of Greek coffee. It was a million miles from Starbucks. I couldn't have been happier. I was replete.

And now for that nap.

Even in my sated state I was *compos mentis* enough to sneak back up the stairs and open my door quietly. I collapsed onto the bed and fell into a deep and dribbling slumber. In hindsight, I probably should have set a limit to my nap. I'd always had people to do this for me. As it was I woke late in the night, bright of eye and bushy of tail. After a luxurious pee, no amount of repose could encourage my eyes to close again.

In the end there was nothing for it, I dressed and took to the streets. An almost full moon made the white buildings glow faintly. Nothing and no-one moved. The only sound, the rustle of water gently washing over coarse beach sand.

I headed towards the edge of the village and the path I had spied earlier in the day, the moon lighting my way like some sort of religious beacon, the only thing missing, a choir of angels singing aaaaah. The path to the ruins started near the small, neat and tidy, freshly painted church.

It was like an elephant trail, seeking out the gentlest gradient to wend its way upwards. Huge stones, worn smooth from the tread of a millenia of foot traffic beckoned me higher. I still didn't know what the ruins represented. I hadn't asked. No doubt it held some sort of religious significance. Probably an alter for sacrificing virgins. They seemed to like that sort of thing. Anyway it might help to inspire my writing, whatever it was.

But frankly, as I climbed higher, I was getting a little spooked. The church had grown small below me and the twinkling lights of the village seemed a long way off, the harbour a black hole in the darkness. Getting mauled to death by a pack of wolves hadn't been part of my plan. But that was what danced in my head. Did they have wolves in Greece? I held no real fear of goats. But if one of those jumped out in front of me at this point, I suspect I would have soiled myself.

But even for all this, the track lured me on. It was a long walk. It was cool but I was sweating. I rounded another bend in the path and stopped, in awe. It was breathtaking and scary, all at the same time. The moon shone through the remaining half-dozen or so columns still standing atop a stone platform. It gave the place a mystical aura. I don't have a religious bone in my body, in fact I had the complete set of anti-Christian bones, but something about this place made me sense a presence, beyond the mortal.

And at that moment I swear I heard something. A noise in the bush. There was only the barest hint of a breeze, so it couldn't have been the wind. I froze, holding my breath. Which was hard to do, given I was still puffing, and sweating, from the climb—it was the most exercise I had done in years.

I needed to breathe again so I slowly exhaled but then paused, holding my breath again, to listen. Nothing. I wanted to climb up into the area between the columns but my feet were frozen to the spot. In the end I backed away, slowly, like you would from a dangerous snake or a jilted lover, never taking your eyes off it/her, no sudden moves.

My heart-rate was higher than it had been on the climb. I eased myself back onto the path before turning and striding with purpose down the hillside. And then I had that awful feeling that something was gaining on me. Like when I was a kid and we had an outside toilet. How many times on the sprint back to the house late at night did I think that something almost had hold of me. Only thwarted by the slamming of the back door.

That's how I felt. I descended far more quickly than was prudent. The path was rough in places and I risked a twisted ankle or worse. But fear is a marvellous motivator. Once the long switchback-turns started I was able to see if anything was behind me, that no sabre-toothed demon was in my wake. I backed off the pace a bit. But not much.

I breathed a sigh of relief as I came to the church. And then something jumped out at me. My heart nearly gave out. I farted. A dog. It growled and ran towards the village, more frightened than me.

"Holy fuckin' shit." I leant briefly against the wall of the church, my legs threatening to buckle beneath me. By the time I got back to the hotel I could see a faint glimmer of the sunrise to come. I'd been gone for hours. I was in a lather of sweat. I fell across my bed into a deep sleep.

3

Alfio was up at dawn as he was on most days. He loved this time of day. His mother would rise when she heard him and it made him smile. He worked quickly to get the kindling to light the fire in the kitchen stove, so he could get the kettle boiling for their morning cup of tea together.

His sisters would be asleep for at least another hour, or longer if they had their way. He smiled again, thinking about how he would wake them so they could be ready for school. Alfio was fourteen but didn't go to school. He was slow. He knew that. He had tried school and didn't like it. He liked to be in the hills with his goats and the other animals, and his mother. His mother had wanted him to be like the other kids in the village, to have an education, but she soon realised that it wasn't to be.

She decided his happiness was more important, so she let him stay home to help. And quickly realised what a great help he was. Never a complaint, never a moan about working hard. Alfio thrived on hard work. But what he loved most was roaming the mountains with the small herd of goats.

A couple of days a week, after milking the herd, Alfio would take to the hills for most of the day with the goats, under the pretext of ensuring they were well fed. His mother would smilingly chide him, saying that he only used his goats as an excuse to roam the mountains.

On the other days he would stay at home and help his mother with chores around their small farm, tending their chickens and sheep. The sheep were the mainstay of their income, the lambs sought-after in the island's restaurants.

They also sold goat cheese and meat. The income was enough to ensure Alfio's sisters would be able to go to boarding school and then on to university. Alfio's mother wanted a better life for her daughters. A life beyond marriage and children.

With the herd milked and the chores done Alfio headed out with the goats. His mother warned him to stay safe, as she did each time. It was more of a standing joke between them, his mother having long-since given up worrying about her son. He was as sure-footed as his charges, and knew every inch of the territory for many kilometres in any direction.

On this day Alfio decided to head north into the hills bordering his village. The country was rough and steep, all limestone boulders and tortured, twisted scrub. He talked quietly to his charges urging them up the faint trails that he knew so well, the tinkling of the bells the only sound beside the gentle breeze rustling the leaves. He would tap his stick on a rock when he was calling for attention, and they would comply readily.

He moved them over a ridge-line and down into the valley beyond. The sun was climbing and the glare from the rocks already enough to make him squint. He forced the pace down into the valley bottom where he knew the animals would enjoy picking in the shade of the trees. There was also a small spring where they could water.

This was one of his favourite places but he was careful not to over-graze any one area, and so it had been almost a month since his previous visit. He found a comfortable spot in the shade and sat to enjoy some bread, olives and cheese from the blue cloth he carried. He took a long drink from the spring and lay quietly under a tree.

As he sometimes did, he drifted into sleep. But on this occasion he slept much longer than usual, waking several hours later, in the mid afternoon. The herd had wandered off. He wasn't particularly concerned. He knew they would work their way along the line of trees that ran up a small side-valley. He had taken them there before. He set off in their wake and quickly picked up their trail.

They had wandered further than he had anticipated, finding the herd more than an hour later. He became concerned when he realised that not all the herd were there. It was the young mother, the black one with the white ring on one eye, and her kid. They were newcomers to the herd, Alfio's mother having traded for the pair only recently. This was their first outing. Alfio felt a little ashamed. He should have been more attentive.

The valley ended against the steep slope of another range. Boulders and twisted scrub barred the way. Alfio knew she wouldn't have gone that way. He left the main herd where they were and headed up the side of the valley with the most vegetation, following a natural trail through the scrub. When he reached the ridge line he had a clear view into the next valley. It was a distant tinkling of a bell that told Alfio he had chosen the right route. He couldn't see the goat but he knew she was somewhere on the opposite side of the next valley.

Alfio knew this meant he would be late home. A worry for his mother. But he couldn't leave the two goats behind. He moved quickly down to the valley floor, choosing a more direct, but rougher, route, scratching his leg on some brambles in the process.

He spotted the trail he knew the mother goat would have taken and headed up. He had moved a distance, following the mother and baby goat and knew that he was closer to the port village than his own. He also knew what lay over the next ridge, the ancient ruins. He had been there a couple of times.

When he started his ascent up the ridge, the sun had already disappeared behind the hills. He was just below the ridge line when he heard the bell tinkle ahead of him. He found the pair standing on the trail that led to the ruins, the outline of which he could make out in the distance. As he was about to guide the goats back down the hillside to begin the long journey home, something caught his eye.

It was a flashlight coming from the ruins. In fact there were two. He knew he had to get home. He was already in trouble, but his curiosity got the better of him. He moved down the track towards the ruins. The track he was on, lead back to the north linking with one of the island's main roads. The track to the port village lay on the other side of the ruins down the mountainside.

He approached the lights without fear or caution. Even so he was almost beside the first man before he was noticed.

"Holy shit," the man said, jumping in fright when he turned to see Alfio standing beside him, a smile on his face.

"Where did he come from?" the second man demanded.

"No idea. Look at him, he must be with the goats we heard before."

Both men had their flashlights pointed into the boy's face, forcing him to shield his eyes. He was still smiling.

"Do you speak English?" asked the taller of the two men.

Alfio smiled and started explaining in Greek about his lost goats.

"I don't think he's real bright."

"What do we do with him?"

"We can't let him go. It's gonna take us a couple of hours to move these pieces. What if he goes down to the village and tells someone before we're finished? Let's take him down the side a bit and tie him up until we're finished." The man tossed his accomplice a length of thin rope. The boy was watching the conversation with interest. He didn't see a lot of foreigners in his small village and the strange words they used brought a smile to his face. He went happily with the tall man off the side of the site, held by the wrist. It wasn't until the man pulled his arms behind his back that the boy became concerned. He pulled against the man's efforts.

"Listen you little prick," said the man, "settle down." He cuffed the boy on the side of the head for good measure. Alfio yelled and struggled more. He didn't like to be held for long. Even his mother could only cuddle him briefly before he would try to break away. The man was trying to wrap the rope around the boy's wrists but was struggling to make headway against Alfio's efforts to resist.

The man was not patient and didn't have much love for anyone or anything. He quickly reached the end of his tether and punched the boy in the side of the head with a bunched fist. But rather than quiet Alfio, it only seemed to goad him into greater action.

"Stan, give me a hand down here will ya."

"Don't use my fuckin' name, you idiot," he yelled back.

But before Stan could get down to where Alfio and the other man were struggling, Alfio broke away and ran into the trees.

"Fuck, he's away," yelled the man. "Head back up the track, and see if you can see him."

Alfio was in a blind panic. He didn't even feel the blow to the side of his head, such was his desperation to be released. He knew he had to get away and back to his goats and his mother. He ran along the side of the steep hill, stumbling several times in the dark. He could hear the man yelling behind him and the other man up above. He ran as fast as he could. With the darkness and his haste he missed the faint trail he had followed up the side of the hill to find his goats. He ran blindly through the darkness struggling to stay on his feet.

The two pursuers had long since lost the boy in the darkness. The man who had attempted to tie the boy had become lost in the trees. He yelled to his accomplice and then spent the next ten minutes battling his way up to the main trail. He was sweating and had more than a few scratches on his face and arms for his efforts.

"Bollocks to that, let's get back and get the job done."

"What if he tells someone before we're finished?"

"What would you rather face. A Greek cop or having to tell that bitch that we didn't get them."

"Let's move them both away from here, up the track a bit, and that way we don't have to come back to this shitty place."

"Orright, but let's double check we've got the right ones."

Stan pulled out his phone and re-checked the photos that the woman had sent to them, against the pieces on the ground.

"Yep, these are the right ones, let's get it done."

The two carvings were heavy. Each required the two men to lift, so it would mean two trips to the vehicle which was parked a couple of kilometres away where the road ended.

The men hefted the first carving, moving it along the track several hundred metres before returning for the second piece.

"Fuckin' heavy shit," said the tall man. "Who's fuckin' idea was this?"

"Errol, shut up and get on with it. This place gives me the creeps."

The men had to stop for breaks along the way. When they got the first piece to the van they rolled out the thick matting, as instructed, to ensure the stones did not suffer damage during the drive back to town.

Then they headed back down the track for the second piece. The moon was well up during the walk back to the ruins. They turned off the torches, finding it easier to see by the bright moonlight. It was a fortuitous turn of events, because someone was at the ruins when they returned.

They saw the man as they turned a bend in the track at the point where they had stashed the second piece.

"That's not the kid," whispered Errol.

"Reckon he's told someone already?"

"Let's just see what he does."

They squatted in the moon-shadow of the trees. After a short time the man turned and headed back down the track on the far side of the ruins towards the port village below. Once he was well out of sight they stood.

"Let's get out of here."

When they got the second stone back to the van they drove back along the track to the island's single arterial road, turning towards the main town in the centre of the island. They parked at a house in a backstreet, one of the few with a garage.

Alfio was in a blind panic. He ran along the side of the hill beyond the valley he had come up. As far as he was concerned the two men were still chasing him. He eventually turned down the hillside and into one of the valleys beyond. He slowed to a walk, his chest heaving from his efforts. He knew he was lost, recognising nothing of the landscape around him. He headed down into the valley hoping he would find something familiar to guide him home. He had to find the goats and get home to his mother.

The moon had not yet risen. It was very dark in the rough scrub on the mountain side. Alfio stepped around a tree and into mid air. He didn't utter a sound as he fell.

The next day Errol and Stan met the woman, as agreed, at the edge of the village. They explained what had happened the previous night.

"You idiots. So you were seen by one, and potentially two people. That's great. What sort of fools did your boss give me." It wasn't a question.

"Look, it was only the kid who saw us," said Errol. "The other bloke didn't, I'm sure about that. And the kid looked pretty dopey and we had our lights in his face. I doubt he'd be able to describe us."

"For your sake, I hope not. You better have looked after those pieces."

Both men nodded.

"There's one more to get. I'll take you to see it tomorrow and then we can get them out of here. I'll call when I want something. Stay in the house, except for meals, and don't do anything stupid. No drinking."

She turned and walked off without another word.

"Bitch," was all Errol said as he started the van.

The woman walked back into the port village, wondering who the man could have been.

4

It was almost lunch time when I woke. I was still dressed in the clothes I had worn up to the ruins.

I showered and dressed again. At this rate I'd need to get some washing done. I eased myself quietly out of my room, to no avail. Aphrodite came storming around the corner.

"Good morning Mr Terry."

My initial annoyance at being ambushed withered as I saw the look of concern on her face.

"Is something wrong?"

"Is very sad today, Mr Terry. A young boy—how you say, a slow boy," she pointed to her head, "from the next village is go missing. He go out yesterday with the goats and he not come home. Many are looking. Is bad. I must go and check with people."

"Sorry, yes, you go."

I walked to the taverna where I'd eaten on the previous day. I could see a few small groups of locals talking together in the street. When the owner came, she, like Aphrodite, looked concerned. I asked where the boy had gone missing, a tingle of apprehension, building in my bones. The woman explained that the boy had been heading further into the mountains from his village. I decided not to say anything about my night-time meander and what I thought I'd heard.

I tried the goat for lunch and chased it down with another small carafe of cheeky local white. No beer this time, I needed to get into some work. I decided goat was a little gamey for my tastes. I sat facing towards the hills and could see a faint outline of the ruins in the distance. It gave me a strange feeling that was hard to shift. As I sat drinking my Greek coffee, I decided I wouldn't be able to get any work done until I put my curiosity to rest.

I paid and went and bought myself a hat and a bottle of water at a nearby tourist shop and headed back towards the small church. The only hat they had that would fit my big head was like the tea-towels my mother would bring home from our rare holidays away from home. It had a series of pictures of island vistas and a big Greek flag across the back.

It was early afternoon, the warmest part of the day. And while it was not mid-summer hot it was enough to bring out the sweat before I had even hit the track. I stopped after a couple of switchback turns to take a slug from the bottle, amazed at what I had done the night before. I could already feel a chafe between my legs.

The view down over the church and the water was splendid. A ferry was entering the harbour. It killed a bit of the rustic beauty, painted by the small fishing boats tethered to their moorings, but the sight of the big boat seemed somehow just as Greek.

I continued to climb, thankful I had bought the hat and water. When I turned the final bend my legs were rubbery, my breath coming in short sharp bursts. I paused in the same spot as the previous night. There was no-one else around. The breeze was much stronger, rustling the dry grasses and scrub that grew around and through the site.

The platform didn't hold the same fear I'd experienced the previous night and I climbed up. It was made up of large slabs of rock and, even after centuries, was still largely square in its dimensions. A number of columns had collapsed, the stone laying in rough piles here and there. To the sides of the main construction were the remnants of other smaller buildings which looked like they were long-ago reduced to low walls and rock piles. Dried grass growing out of, and around, the piles waved in the afternoon breeze.

I wandered the site, doing a loop beyond its outer perimeter, still with the belief I had heard something the previous night. I walked down off the side of the site to a small stand of stunted trees. It was steep, and the shaley rocks were skittery under foot. I had to grab a tree branch to steady myself. I decided I was now being silly and turned to fight my way back up the slope, before I really injured myself or was bitten by a snake. Did they have snakes in Greece? Maybe a Pythagoras.

If I hadn't slipped and almost fallen flat on my big arse, arms windmilling in an effort to grab a tree branch, I would have missed it. At the base of the tree was a piece of rope. I bent down to retrieve it. It was then I saw the broken silver bracelet with the cross on it.

"Curiouser and curiouser said Alice," I said out loud.

I put both rope and bracelet in my pocket, had a last look around the site and started down the hill. When I arrived back at the hotel Aphrodite was sitting at the front desk. She looked crushed.

"Mr Terry, the news is very bad. They find the boy. He is dead. They say he is fallen in a bad place, into the rock. It is very sad."

When I asked where they found him, she pointed to a map of the

25

island, hanging on the wall. It was a point, some distance from the ruins, but not as far north as she'd suggested earlier.

Still.

I said nothing about what I'd found or my escapade. I was hot and tired. I knew I wouldn't get anything done in this condition at this time of day, so I went to my room and changed into my swim gear and headed down to the beach to wash away the grime.

A couple of families were on the beach. I dumped my gear and wandered into the water, looking down at my pasty white, flabby stomach. Not pretty. A few more reps of that bloody hill will take care of it. I was the only one out in a swimming depth. I wondered what lurked in Mediterranean waters. Coming from Australia made you think of these things. Are there sharks in Greece? I didn't fear the octopus. In fact, I intended reeking havoc on their population later at the dinner table.

I smiled at a mother on the beach who looked my way.

"Althaia says you're a famous author." She had a toffee English accent.

"I'm sorry, who's Althaia?"

"The woman who owns the hotel. We're staying there as well."

"Ah, Aphrodite."

She gave me a quizzical look.

"The goddess of love. She's quite a fan."

The woman laughed. Her face lit up. She was very pretty. Dark hair, flawless skin, and nice long, brown legs. Good muscle tone.

"I haven't read any of your work. What is your genre?"

Warning. When they started using words like 'genre' I was skeptical that they would be fans of my work. I'd been caught before.

"Contemporary fiction." My go-to phrase for these scenarios.

"Are you here to relax or work?"

"A bit of both. And you, you're with your family?"

"Yes, those two trying to drown each other, over there, are mine."

"Nice."

"Have you been up to the ruins yet?"

"A couple of times actually. Once on the first night, when I couldn't sleep, and today as well.

She gave me a strange look.

"Well, I'd better get the children back to the hotel for a shower before dinner. Might see you around."

"Absolutely."

I watched her walk down to her kids. Nice legs indeed. She smiled as she walked back past me, heading towards the hotel.

I sat on the hotel towel enjoying the last of the afternoon rays. I couldn't help but look back up the hill towards the ruins. I really should take the rope and the bracelet to the cops, or whatever they have here. No, I'm just being stupid. The bracelet could belong to any of the thousands of tourists who have traipsed around the ruins. The boy wasn't found there. It can't be connected. I'd look silly. I gathered up my stuff and headed back to the hotel. Time for a shower and then off to fulfil my commitment to lower the octopus population.

Aphrodite had recovered some of her good form, ambushing me inside the front door.

"Mr Terry, Mr Terry, where you eat tonight? My friend Voula, she is big fan like me, she has a restaurant and would love to meet with you. I can take you for dinner. You no pay."

She was like a giggly school girl.

"Thanks, but I already have plans this evening." Nothing was going to spoil my octopus. But even I couldn't help to be a little moved by the crestfallen look on her face.

"Perhaps another night." It's all that was required. A little ray of hope started to dance across her substantial jowl.

"Yes, yes. We do it tomorrow night. I tell Voula. Her food is best. You will love her lamb. She make it traditional. Very delicious."

She turned and all-but sprinted away before I had a chance to say anything. I had my shower and then stood naked in front of the open doors leading to my small balcony. The sun was gone and the lights started to dance on the smooth waters of the harbour. I looked down at my desk at the piece of rope and bracelet sitting on my note book. The bracelet was made of small, fine links with a simple silver cross. It looked cheap, like something a kid would wear.

I headed off to my taverna-of-choice and was greeted warmly by the owner. She knows she's on to a good thing seeing me again. Lucky for her I'm a creature of habit. I was sipping on some frosty amber nectar—the octopus already being slaughtered out the back—when the yummy mummy from the beach sat down at a table nearby with her sprogs. She smiled when she saw me.

It was a nice smile. Great teeth. Good skin. And her most important attribute, no hubby.

"Hello."

"Hello yourself."

"I hope my children don't ruin your serenity."

"No, I love kids," I nearly gagged on the words. I was tempted to ask her to join me but I was really looking forward to giving uninterrupted attention to my grilled octopus salad. And so it was a shock when Maria—we were now on a first-name basis—brought my plate. I was expecting a plethora of the little buggers. Instead I got one, very large tentacle. My first thought was, I went swimming with these things.

"Maria, it's huge. Are they all this big?"

Maria laughed as she walked away, shaking her head.

It was divine. Lightly grilled over charcoal with lemon juice, Maria told me.

She'd convinced me that I should wash it down with raki and who was I to argue with ancient customs. By the time I was finished the octopus I was on my fourth glass and feeling very well disposed towards my fellow man, or more importantly, woman. I looked across at the yummy mummy, as she was rising from her table.

"Why don't you come back for a drink. This raki is fantastic."

"Unfortunately I can't leave these two alone."

"I'm sure Aphrodite can find someone to watch them for an hour."

"Thank you, but they can be a little challenging at bed-time. Perhaps some other time."

Her tone was still friendly but I got the distinct impression I'd been brushed. I turned to survey the few other tables with customers. Couples, and all old farts. No action here tonight.

Maria brought me a coffee and some halva. I was pondering whether to kick on and see what options might present themselves at the other tavernas, when the light was blocked out in front of me. It was like an eclipse.

He was the tallest Greek I had ever seen. His head was the size of a piano accordion complete with a keyboard of white teeth. His handlebar moustache was so big it could have swept an Australian country dance hall clean, in one pass. I'm sure I had seen him in World War Two movies where English commandos worked with Greek partisans in the hills of Crete to thwart the Nazi invaders. He was the quiet bloke, the one whose family had been killed by the Germans. The only thing he had left to love was his big knife, whose blade he continually honed to a surgical sharpness, all the better for severing Kraut jugulars. And his name was always Stavros.

He said nothing for what seemed an eternity. I was too flummoxed—and a little too drunk—to think of anything to say.

"You are writer." It was a statement. I still had nothing to add. I was staring dumbly at the scar that ran from the corner of his eye down across his cheek.

"I am Stavros."

He reached one of his paws towards me. It was the size of a baseball catcher's mitt. My hand disappeared into its vastness. I tensed, waiting for the sound of crunching bones. It didn't happen. While his hand felt like dried-out leather, his touch was gentle. He smiled, showing me that his bottom teeth were a carbon copy of the top. He sat.

"I feesh."

"You feesh…?"

"Nay, I feesh."

"You mean you fish?"

"Nay."

"You don't fish."

"I feesh."

"You fish?"

"Nay."

I was locked in the Greek version of 'who's-on-first?' I was sobering quickly.

Thankfully Maria chose to come out at this time.

"Nay in Greek means yes. Stavros means he is fisherman."

"Nay, I feesh." He continued to smile, nodding in agreement.

I felt worn out.

"I read book."

Oh god, he wants to keep talking.

"I read in Greek. You write in Greek." He scrunched his eye-brow—singular—giving me a quizzical look. "How come you no speak in Greek?"

"Maria." I yelled at her disappearing back. "Please, Maria. Please explain that my books are translated into other languages, by someone else." Maria prattled on with Stavros for some time. Eventually the huge head nodded in understanding. She turned to me.

"The octopus you eat for dinner, Stavros catch this."

He smiled, looking very pleased.

"I feesh."

"Yes, yes you do."

"You come feesh with me."

I started to explain that, while that sounded nice, I would need to check my schedule. He interrupted.

"I get you tomorrow, five o'clock," he said it with finality, adding, "you stay Althaia hotel. Althaia tell me room. I get you."

Oh god. I nodded. He rose, ducking under the roof structure, straightening only when he was outside. He disappeared quickly into the darkness of a side street. I gave up on the idea of more alcohol and the potential for adult entertainment and headed back to my room. Tomorrow promised to be an interesting day. I needed sleep if I was to be dragged out of bed by the hulking Stavros at some ungodly hour.

5

I'd tossed and turned most of the night, wondering what I'd gotten myself into. When Stavros pounded on the door I felt like I'd had about ten minutes sleep. I thought about ignoring him but figured he'd pull the door off its hinges.

I plodded over in my boxer shorts.

"You dress. We go," was all he said. He waited patiently in the hall while I threw on some clothes. He gave a grunt of approval when I re-appeared a few minutes later with my hat.

"You come." He waggled his fingers behind him, like he was leaving a trail of crumbs for me to follow as he headed down the stairs and into the deserted village streets.

We walked down to the break-water, through the faint light cast by a couple of widely spaced street lights, and down some old stone stairs to a lower level against which Stavros' dory was tied. The wooden boat wasn't much bigger than a good-sized dinghy. It had a tiny wheelhouse in the centre. It was very neat and tidy. Ropes and nets were rolled and folded, and packed. Every surface or implement that could be painted was either a shiny clean white or a Mediterranean blue. The floor space was as uncluttered as it could be. Stavros was evidently house-proud.

He pointed to the side of the boat, "you sit," wanting me out of the way while he went about his business, checking this and winding up that. Then he disappeared into the tiny door near the steering wheel. After a minute or so I could hear the quiet chug-chugging of the boat's engine.

Stavros reappeared. He pointed to the front. "Undo rope."

I went forward to where a rope, connected to the front of the boat, was tied to an old wooden bollard on the landing jetty. The knot looked complicated. I panicked. I tugged and heaved, but to no avail. Stavros came forward, took the rope, gave it a flick and a light tap and it miraculously undid itself. He smiled at me, rolled the rope and stored it away.

He waggled his fingers and I followed him back to the wheel where he pushed a lever forward. The engine chugged a little harder and we began to move gently forwards, turning in a big lazy arc, heading back towards the end of the break-water and the harbour entrance. He pointed the little boat towards the open sea, pushed the throttle open further and then stepped away from the wheel.

"You take."

I jumped behind the wheel. He leaned a huge arm over my shoulder and pointed.

"This star, you drive." The star was easy to see, much brighter than those around it and not far above the horizon. I smiled to myself as Stavros stepped away to go about his business. Despite the lack of sleep I was enjoying my outing with the giant Greek. The morning was perfectly still, the water oily smooth. There was a hint of red in the sky off to the left. Port maybe, I thought, smiling again.

My boating experiences were minimal, restricted to a cruise I'd been invited on, at the height of my publishing powers. The guest speaker on a literary cruise, where I'd been fawned over and spent much of the time drinking expensive wines, or recovering from drinking expensive wines. I smiled again. I think I was enjoying this more.

Stavros had his big head stuck through the little cabin door. When he turned he was carrying two huge white mugs in one hand and two small glasses in the other. He placed them on a shelf in front of the wheel and then passed me a small glass, holding his own to his lips.

"Yamas."

"Yamas," I responded downing the liquid. The aroma hit my nose before it touched my tongue. Ouzo. One of those drinks that smelled wonderful but whose taste didn't quite match the expectation. But here aboard a smart little octopus boat chugging out into the Mediterranean with the promise of a wonderful sunrise in the offing, it seemed pretty bloody good.

Stavros smiled and took my glass.

"Drink coffee."

I took up the big mug and sipped. It was steaming hot, white and sweet. Divine.

We didn't say much to each other as we chugged along. Stavros was busy readying his gear. I happily steered the boat. Half an hour later we were off the coast of another small island, which I could see—to paraphrase Homer—thanks to dawn's rosy red fingers spreading across the ocean. Stavros came back and took over the wheel, slowing the boat, steering along the island's coastline.

He stopped near a buoy, the little boat bobbing when its wake passed under the hull. He took up a long, hooked pole which he used to pull the buoy into the boat along with the rope attached to it. He hauled on the rope, hand over hand, and pulled in two lengths of white PVC pipe about a metre long, upending them into a plastic bin. Two huge octopus tumbled into the bottom. Yep, this is what I'd eaten at Maria's. No more swimming for me. They were huge and constantly moving, slithering.

He returned the traps to the water and we moved on to the next buoy. As we pulled beside another buoy I tapped his arm.

"Me, this time," and pointed at the buoy.

He smiled.

I took the long hook and after several attempts managed to snag the line as the boat gently rocked in the fat, lazy swell. As I started to haul on the wet rope I realised how much the water-filled PVC weighed. It was hard work, the rope coarse against my soft hands. Thankfully the water wasn't deep. I pulled the pipes up to the edge of the boat, water draining from a small hole bored into each. Stavros was beside me but did not help. With most of the water drained I upended the pipes into the bin. Two more octopus tumbled out.

Stavros clapped me on the back with a huge paw.

"Good, writer, good. You feesh."

"Nay, I feesh," I said in return. We both laughed.

The sun climbed and we worked our way around the tiny island. Stopping frequently to haul in the traps. Stavros didn't let me do too many more. He could see my hands were already sore and my shoulders weak. I was a little embarrassed.

When we reached the far side of the island Stavros pulled into a small cove, running up alongside an old rotting jetty. It was a stunning vista. The sun was well up by this time and I could see into the depths of the clear water, teaming with fish life.

Stavros shut down the engine and tied off the boat. He grabbed a bag from the cabin, bidding me follow with his waggling fingers.

We stepped off the jetty onto a path through the few trees that bordered the rocky shore. Behind the trees was a small clearing with an old single-room cabin, tired and dilapidated. The windows were gone, the front door hung askew, and many of the roof tiles were broken.

We didn't go into the cabin. Stavros headed towards a circle of stones out front.

"You sit."

He put his bag down and went off through the trees, returning after a few minutes with an armful of wood. Within a few minutes he had a fire going and a frying pan sizzling hot. He pulled out a container and removed the lid, tipping octopus into the pan along with the juices in which it had been marinating.

It took only a few minutes to cook. He divided it onto two plates, handing me one, along with a large chunk of bread and cheese. My mouth was watering. I could smell the oil and pepper and other spices. It was divine. And before I had even finished the first mouthful he handed me the mug again, but this time filled with white wine. I sat back and sighed with pleasure.

"Efharisto," I said in my embarrassingly limited Greek.

Stavros smiled.

"You work, you eat," was all he said.

We sat in a companionable silence, the sun peaking over the tops of the nearby trees, sipping and chewing our way through one of the best meals I had ever eaten. We didn't stop for long. I made sure I ran forward to untie the boat without prompting this time. We chugged our way back out of the cove and finished retrieving the final few octopus traps. Stavros smiled when we began the homeward journey.

"Good catch. You make me lucky, writer."

When we got back to the harbour it was early afternoon. The early start and the lack of sleep were beginning to catch up with me. But I realised that the work wasn't finished. For the next hour we stood pounding the octopus against the stone jetty. Stavros explained in his halting English that we needed to remove all the water from the octopus and tenderise it, otherwise it would be tough and no good for cooking. It would also need to be hung for a day, before he sold it.

As much as I wanted to go back to my room I was determined to see the work-day through. I'm not sure what Stavros expected me to do, but he seemed to take delight in showing me how to manage the catch. Eventually he hoisted the huge tub onto his shoulder and we headed off towards the hotel. He stopped at a side street, near the *Cycladaen*.

"Thank you, writer," he said, reaching out his massive hand.

"No, thank you."

With that he headed off up the hill.

Aphrodite was standing near the front door of the hotel when I walked through. She smiled when she saw me.

"You are Greek fisherman."

"Nay." I laughed. "I am a tired Greek fisherman who needs a shower."

"Please, you bring me your clothes to wash."

I thought this an odd thing to say but then realised I must smell like Stavros.

"Yes. Afharisto."

"I knock on your door at seven to go to dinner to Voula restaurant."

Shit, I'd forgotten. I saw that she saw the look on my face.

"You are still come?"

I was knackered. I wanted a quiet one. But that look on her face. I smiled.

"Of course I'm coming."

She beamed.

I still had a couple of hours to recline from my day of labour. I opened the door to my room and sensed straight away that something was amiss. The balcony doors were open. I know I had closed and locked them. I panicked, thinking that my laptop and camera might be gone but both were sitting on the bedside table where I had left them. It took me a few seconds to realise that the only things missing were the rope and the bracelet. I'd left them on top of my note pad and now they were gone. I sat on the bed. Holy shit. This was getting weird.

6

Errol and Stan were parked at the edge of the village in the white van, as they had been told to do by the woman. Neither man liked the woman but they knew she was well-connected with their boss and so treated her—to her face, at least—with respect.

She made them wait a long time, the heat in the vehicle making them sweat. It wasn't the only thing that made them sweat, they were worried by the death of the kid. Stan, particularly, was troubled by it. They knew it must be the boy they had attempted to tie up, and even though they'd not killed him, Stan felt a pang of guilt. Stan had values. No women or kids. He drew the line. Anyone else was just business, and there'd been plenty of business over the years.

Errol drew his line in a different place. His main concern was not so much the death of the boy, more the concern of it becoming a police issue. He didn't know much about foreign prisons—he knew quite a bit about English ones—but the bits he'd seen on TV and read about, suggested most of them would not be pleasant places to spend time.

They'd been convinced by the boss in London that this was a straight-forward, sub-contract job. Money for jam, and a nice holiday to boot. Some fuckin' holiday, he'd said to Stan. Not allowed to drink or do anything. And now, the death of a kid had the potential to throw a large spanner in the works.

The two men had talked these things through and were troubled enough to raise it with the woman. She eventually arrived. Before she could say anything, Stan spoke.

"We're a bit concerned about the death of the boy. We heard about it. It must be the one we ran into. Is that going to come back on us?"

Eve turned to eyeball him.

"Look. It's unfortunate. But no-one thinks anything other than it was an accident. There's nothing to be concerned about. And I found out who the man was at the site. He's a tourist. He doesn't seem to know anything. But I want one of you to have a quick look in his room. And then we can get on and get this job done and get out of here."

Eve ran a gallery in London selling sculpture and artworks. And while the gallery did very nicely, she made a much better living trafficking in stolen antiquities for the many wealthy clients around the world who were not concerned about the origins of desirable and desired pieces. She was convinced that many of them were more excited by a piece that was stolen.

She generally worked on commission, finding the pieces that a client was seeking rather than having pieces and seeking a buyer. Eve believed there was a far greater risk in getting caught in the latter scenario. But she had done it on occasion when a great piece fell into her lap.

She'd discovered, moving pieces this way was a bit like laundering money. It was a matter of getting a piece to look clean and legitimate. She had learned that there were ways of doing this. Getting pieces into small galleries in places like the US worked well. These galleries often didn't have the resources or the inclination for a provenance search. An exhibition was a way to 'season' a piece, establish its legitimate bona fides. And then it was a matter of finding a buyer. But people were often queuing to get hold of such pieces.

But typically she worked on commission. Like this case. Where a rich American had wanted some pieces to display in the burgeoning Greek room of his large and rambling home. Eve had visited the house on several occasions, having sourced pieces previously from other countries. She thought the home distasteful and garish. But she kept these things to herself, her focus on the fee.

She was excited by the pieces they taken from the ruins. They weren't significant, but they were just the thing that her buyer in the US was looking for, and he was happy to pay a pretty penny for them. Her client had been specific about what he wanted. Eve had put out feelers with the few contacts she maintained in Greece for such a commission. It didn't take long before a contact responded, suggesting a couple of locations where she might find what she was seeking, complete with photos.

She enjoyed this work. A job like this was a logistical challenge. Putting aside the risk involved, getting the pieces away from the sites and out of the country involved some serious planning and implementation.

And of course, there was the risk factor. The Greeks, like most other countries where she sourced pieces, took a very dim view of people, particularly foreigners, stealing their antiquities and moving them to other countries. Prison sentences were lengthy, fines massive. Eve didn't get a buzz out of the idea that she was flouting the law, as some did. She had her mind on only one thing, to make a lot of money and retire. And this last piece would fulfil her contract with her client and significantly fatten her foreign account.

It wouldn't be much longer before she could pull out of the business and retire somewhere warm with the kids. She had never planned to do it forever. She knew if she kept at it long enough, that somewhere along the way there would be a slip-up. It wouldn't be her slip-up, she was too smart for that. No, it would be some moron like Stan or Errol, or a disgruntled client that would see her in trouble. She wanted to make sure she was out of the business before this happened.

The death of the boy was a slip-up, but staying on and finishing the job was a well-considered risk. She was comfortable that nothing was amiss. The writer hadn't said anything. Eve felt confident that the odds of a good outcome were well in her favour. No, she would stay and finish the job.

She actually enjoyed the writer's company. He wasn't the sharpest knife in the drawer but he was funny and not unattractive. She knew she had him on a string, she just hadn't decided whether to play it through to the obvious conclusion. She'd leave it for now and maybe just enjoy his company.

"Now, which one of you is going to have a look in the writer's room, he's out for the day, so now's the time to do it."

"Stan's good at that stuff," said Errol.

Stan gave his off-sider a filthy look.

"Right, here's my key. Give me five minutes. I'll go back and keep the hotel owner busy. You go into my room and then climb along two balconies and see if you can get his balcony doors open. Just have a look around and then come back here and leave. I'll give you a call."

Eve walked back to the hotel. Althaia was in the foyer with Eve's two children. She stayed there talking to Althaia until she saw Stan walk past heading back towards the van. When she got back to her room she found a piece of rope and bracelet on her bed.

"What has the idiot done!"

7

As tired as I was from my day of labour I couldn't nod off. I lay naked on my bed, my hair damp from the long shower, a breeze ruffling the curtains through the open balcony doors. The thought that someone had been in my room troubled me. I was feeling guilty that I hadn't told anyone about the rope and the bracelet. Did it have a connection to the dead boy? There wasn't much I could do about it now. People would think I was nuts. I drifted off without realising, and was woken by a gentle tapping on the door.

"Mr Terry, Mr Terry, it is time to go."

I was still naked and thought I best not risk my virtue with Aphrodite, so said through the closed door that I would meet her downstairs in a few minutes. Aphrodite gave me a beaming smile when I came down the stairs.

"It is only a small walk."

We turned the corner from the hotel, along the same narrow street up which Stavros had disappeared. It was a short steep climb that plateaued into a small square.

"This is plaka," said Aphrodite, "and Voula restaurant."

The eponymously named establishment was humming. I quickly

realised why, a cheer going up when Aphrodite and I entered through the front door. Apparently it wasn't only the three of us for dinner. I gave a wave and smiled. I was actually touched. It had been a while since I had enjoyed this sort of attention. I was shown to the head of the largest table, but before I sat, everyone stood. I was given a small glass and they toasted me.

"Yamas."

Althaia introduced me to Voula and some of her other friends. I couldn't help but notice—it would have been impossible not too—that Stavros sat in the back corner of the room. I saluted him with my glass and he gave me a shy wave. Voula bid me sit and hurried off to the kitchen. Bread and dips were served.

Over the course of the evening everyone in the room came up to shake my hand and say hello. Some shyly in Greek, with Althaia translating, others in halting English. It was a great night. The lamb was cooked slowly in a clay pot, I was advised by more than a few of those present. It was one of the most tender and succulent meat dishes I had ever eaten.

I drank more than a few glasses of the local red wine. Once again I was feeling very well-disposed towards my fellow human. By the end of the evening everyone was standing and circulating. More than a few selfies were taken with me as the centrepiece. To my dismay, the only person I didn't get to talk to was Stavros, who, when I looked for him, had disappeared. Althaia explained, that Stavros was a shy man who lived by himself, and that I should be honoured that he came to dinner at all. It was apparently a rare occurrence.

I farewelled Voula and her husband with hearty hugs, embarrassing myself in the process by offering them money for the meal. When Althaia and I arrived back at the hotel I thanked her for a wonderful night and gave her a hug. She beamed and bid me good night. It wasn't until I was in my room that I thought again about the dead boy and the missing rope and bracelet.

8

It had taken a few days, but I woke feeling normal. Well-rested and not too much of a hangover. Normal. I dressed and headed to Maria's for breakfast, still feeling a high from the previous night's festivities. And to top it off, my favourite mother was there.

"Morning," I said as I passed the table. After my previous brush-off I decided to play it a little cool.

"Good morning to you, I hear you were quite the hot-ticket item in town last night. Althaia's been talking again."

I laughed.

"Yes, what I understood was a quiet dinner for three turned out to be an intimate gathering for fifty. But, it was a fantastic night."

"One of the benefits of being on the best-seller list, I expect," she said, a hint of a sparkle in her eye.

"Well, it's been a while since I've been in that position, but it was a nice evening none-the-less."

"I'm Eve, by-the-way."

"I'm Terry, nice to meet you."

"Why don't you join me. I've dispatched the urchins to the beach below."

I could see her kids playing on the sand in front of the Taverna.

"Thanks," I said pulling up a chair. "So, you know about me. What do you do?"

"Nothing much, a single mother enjoying a nice break from the rat race of London."

"How long have you been here?"

"I only arrived the day before you."

"And how long will you stay?"

"We'll leave in a few days."

"Have you had a look around the island?"

"No," she paused. "We haven't left the village. But I was thinking about taking the bus to the capital. Interested in a road trip?"

"I was thinking the same thing."

"Don't you need to work?"

"Ah, still researching."

"So, it's a book about this place. Anything you can give away?"

"Nothing to tell yet. Still feeling it out. Seeing if there's anything in it for me."

"Well, that's settled then. The bus leaves at half-ten. I'll see you at the bus stop."

I watched her leave the restaurant and gather her kids. She moved like one of the big cats. Liquid motion, smooth and efficient, and enough leg showing to remind me how splendid they were. I finished breakfast, sitting and enjoying a second coffee.

Eve was right, I did need to do some work. That was why I was here. But I wasn't going to pass up the chance to spend some time with her. I still had plenty of time to knuckle down. And as I'd said to her, a bit of gadding about was good for my research and state of mind. So I went back to my room for my camera, a little excited about a jaunt with her.

It felt strange being this excited. For so long I had taken female interest for granted while my popularity was high. But here I was behaving like a teenager heading out on my first date. It was all a matter of perspective. I wasn't fussed on the idea of having the kids along, not because I wanted her alone, more because my experience with kids had never been positive. The only kids I'd really spent any time with were my step-sister's monsters. One Christmas was enough to enforce an ongoing string of excuses as to why it couldn't possibly ever happen again.

We climbed aboard the old white bus, the kids racing to sit in the bench seat across the rear. They laughed as we chugged our way out of the village and up the climb between two valleys, a plume of black smoke belching behind us.

Apart from one very old Greek woman, all in black, we were the only passengers. The kids thought it a grand adventure, bouncing high on the seat as the bus navigated the winding and bumpy road. The main town was only about twenty kilometres away, with a small village, off on a side road, in between.

"I wonder if this is the village the boy came from, the one who died. Did you hear about that?"

Eve looked at me.

"Yes, I did hear about that, very sad. Sounded like he got lost in the hills."

I was tempted to share my own experience, tell her about the rope and the bracelet. But I thought she might think me crazy, so kept it to myself. We climbed off the bus in the plaka of the island's capital. It was a bigger town than the one where I was staying. The plaka was surrounded by two-storey buildings, several looked official.

"There's a small museum here, I was keen to take a look. Do you mind?"

"No," I said. "Not at all."

I hadn't thought much about what I wanted to do, happy just to tag along with Eve. I wasn't much for museums. I preferred colour and movement, especially the colour of a restaurant menu and the movement of the waiting staff. It was more of a house than any sort of formal building, but it was quaint. The ubiquitous Greek woman in black greeted us enthusiastically at the door and we paid our entrance fee.

"I'm a bit excited," said Eve as we entered. "They have a couple of friezes here that I've read about, from the classical period.

She found them straight away and seemed awe-struck. She talked to me but never took her eyes off the scratched rocks. The kids had run off into another room, but she seemed not to notice.

"These are marvellous. They only found them in the last twenty years, the condition is spectacular. They would be at home in any country's most important museum. I know the Acropolis museum in Athens is keen to get hold of them. Stunning, simply stunning."

I didn't have a lot to add. I didn't want to break her obvious fascination, especially to say something lame.

"I'll check on the kids," I said thinking of something useful to do.

I found them with the old Greek lady in another room who had them seated and was plying them with lollies. She gave me a big smile when I entered.

"Beautiful, beautiful," she said.

I couldn't be bothered explaining that they weren't mine. Eve came trotting in shortly after.

"I'm very sorry," she said to the old woman, "I was a bit distracted by the wonderful friezes."

She seemed genuinely embarrassed.

"Beautiful, beautiful," the old woman repeated running her hand through the blond hair of one of the kids.

We looked at the rest of the house but returned again to the friezes, for a final pause before stepping outside.

"They really are wonderful pieces," was the first thing she said. "I can't believe they keep them here. They are so rare and valuable."

"You have a background with this sort of stuff?"

"I have a small gallery in London selling art and sculpture. It's scary to think what they would be worth," she said pointing back towards the house. "Sorry for being a bit vague back there, I was quite taken."

"Yeah, I kind of noticed. Nice to see someone with a passion."

We found a cafe off the plaka and bought the kids ice creams and ourselves a coffee. Afterwards we wandered the streets, looking through the tourist shops and admiring the views from the town, which was perched high up in the hills. It was possible to see the ocean in several directions.

The bus passed through again at lunch time and we returned to the port village. We lunched at Maria's on return.

"The kids want to play on the beach this afternoon. Come along if you feel like it."

I was sorely tempted to keep the day going, ever hopeful that it might lead somewhere for me. But even with this I knew I had to start doing some work. As nice as it was being here with Eve, I reminded myself how I was going to feel if I went home without some sort of progress on my writing. It was my last chance.

"I'd love to but I'd better get some work done."

I paid the bill and headed back to my room. I stopped for a quick hello with Althaia and then headed upstairs. I seated myself, after opening the balcony doors, and lifted the laptop lid. I tried not to think about that sense of foreboding I'd had the last fifty times I had gone through this process. I didn't have a plan or even an idea. This was as it had always been. Things would come.

I thought I'd start with a short piece on the trip so far. Something to get me going again. An *amuse bouche*, to get the juices flowing. I started typing, the words came slowly but built gradually. Before long I was enjoying myself.

9

I'd been at it for a couple of hours, when there was a polite knock at the door. I thought about ignoring it. I was on a bit of a roll. It wasn't my next book but it still felt good for the words to flow. It had been a while since I felt this way. But the knock came again. I thought it might be Althaia, and was surprised to see the hallway filled by my huge fisherman friend.

"Stavros, kalimera."

His big white teeth lit up the darkened hallway as he smiled.

"Writer, hello. You work?" He gave a concerned look when he spied my open laptop on the desk.

"Is ok," I replied, using the poor grammar of someone trying to communicate in their own language with someone who didn't understand it very well.

"Come, we drink coffee and ouzo."

It was late afternoon, and I had been a good boy. I deserved a reward.

"Okay. Maria's?

"Yes, Maria."

"I'll have a quick shower and see you there."

Stavros nodded his understanding, turned on his heel and headed to the stairs. I could hear him humming a tune I didn't recognise. I showered and dressed in clean clothes—all my clothes had been freshly laundered and returned to me, courtesy of Althaia. Stavros was sitting with Maria and her husband when I arrived.

It was another stunning afternoon in paradise. A gentle breeze made the high-tide water slap softly against the concrete wall at my feet. The sun was already behind the hills, a red glow basting the harbour and village. I could see Eve and her kids and a couple of other families further along the bay, playing in the shallows. I smiled at my new friends, who welcomed me warmly to their table.

"Sit, sit," said Maria. "Coffee and ouzo?"

"That would be fantastic, Maria."

Maria's husband, Petros, was even more shy than Stavros. He smiled at me and nodded but would make no effort to speak anything other than his native tongue. Stavros clapped me on the shoulder, sending a shock-wave through my whole body, rattling my eye-balls in their sockets. He laughed and proceeded to go into a long diatribe with Petros in Greek.

"I tell, you are fisherman, not writer."

We all laughed together in a melange of multicultural and multilingual mastication. Maria brought my coffee and ouzo and I sat with my two Greek friends, answering the occasional question but mostly nodding and smiling as the two men spoke together. I was very happy.

Eve walked in with the children. They'd been home to shower and were having an early dinner. She stopped at my table and said hello to the other men and me.

"You're practically a local now."

"So it would seem," I said. "There are worse things."

She laughed and took her kids to a table in the corner.

As darkness settled over the village Stavros bid me good night and headed home. Petros headed to the kitchen to begin his night's work. I finished my ouzo and moved to Eve's table. The children had finished their dinner.

"We're heading off. Give me twenty minutes to get the kids into bed and come over. I've got a bottle of red. We can have a glass on the balcony."

I took a short stroll down along the break-water. I could see Stavros' boat sitting among the others of the local fleet. There was not a breath of wind. The lights of the village were reflected on the smooth water. I sat on one of the big rocks that formed the break-water. It was the dead boy and the bracelet which came to mind. I'd started to believe that I was looking for a conspiracy where there was none. Why would someone want to murder an autistic kid anyway. It didn't make much sense. He couldn't have been a threat to anybody. The bracelet could've belonged to a stupid tourist, someone like me who fell flat on their arse going somewhere they shouldn't have.

And it could have been the room cleaner who took the bracelet, or maybe they had a kid with them who pocketed it. That would make more sense. It was a cheap piece of crap. Some kid probably took it. And it was probably the cleaner who left the balcony doors open. I felt satisfied with my conclusions. I really didn't want this in my head any longer. I made an agreement with myself not to think about it any more.

I headed back to the hotel, anticipating a quiet drink with Eve. I didn't know what to expect. Wild sex in the same room as her kids was most likely off the table. But strangely I had stopped thinking about her in this way. It wasn't that I didn't want her, no, the subtlest of nods from her would have had me prancing around like a stud stallion. I just wasn't overly concerned about whether it would happen.

My god, what was this island doing to me? I wasn't maturing, was I? Heaven forbid that I might enjoy a woman's company. I laughed out loud as I headed up the stairs of the hotel. Eve's room was only two doors along from mine. I knocked lightly. The door opened quietly and Eve put a finger to her lips. Both kids were out to it.

She beckoned that I follow and we stepped out onto the small balcony. There was just enough room for the small wrought-iron table and two matching chairs. Eve had set out the bottle and two glasses and even some snacks.

"Sorry about the catering," she laughed. "Doritos was the best I could do at short notice."

"It's a step up from what you would have got from my place."

We laughed again. She poured the wine and we clinked our glasses.

"Yamas," I said.

"Yamas."

We chatted about her gallery in London and about my books. She was a smart woman and made me feel a bit stupid, especially talking about my story plots. I'd never felt apologetic about my work before but in Eve's company I felt like a bit of a dork. Not that she judged me. She was complimentary about what I had achieved.

"Can I use your bathroom, or should I go and use mine?"

She laughed. She had perfect white teeth.

"No, use mine. Nothing will wake them now."

I stepped quietly inside the room. Beside the wall, outside the bathroom was a chair with a teddy bear sitting on it. I did my business in the bathroom and came out again and looked at the bear. Something had caught my eye. Hanging around the bear's neck was a silver bracelet. It can't be. I looked around to see if Eve was looking, but the curtains blocked her view. I picked the bear up and looked more closely. Was it the bracelet? But why would it be here? It didn't make sense. Why would Eve take it?

Perhaps the kids got into my room. But that was unlikely. Maybe it wasn't the same bracelet. This was freaking me out.

"What are you up to?"

She had walked soundlessly into the room. I felt like a thief who had been caught in the act.

"Oh, ah, nothing, just admiring the bear. I had one like it when I was a kid."

Eve gave me a funny look, her head cocked slightly to one side, staring at me intently, like she was running my words through a lie detector. I felt very uncomfortable and stupid, standing there holding a teddy bear.

"It's Hannah's," Eve smiled, the odd expression disappearing, "she never goes anywhere without it." She took the bear from me and placed it back on the chair.

I was tempted to make a comment about the bracelet but thought better of it. What could I say? I had one like it, did your kid steal it?

"Well," I said, "it's getting late, I'll leave you to it. Thanks for the wine."

"You're welcome. Thanks for the company."

As I walked back to my room I analysed our parting. Eve's words seemed genuine and apart from the odd expression on her face earlier, I sensed no change in her attitude towards me. I opened the balcony doors and flopped across my bed. Shit, just when I'd convinced myself that I was making it all up.

10

I woke with a start, not realising that I'd fallen asleep, a commotion coming from the street below. It was a loud voice, yelling in Greek. I paused. I knew that voice. It was Stavros.

I'd fallen asleep in my clothes so only had to pull some shoes on before I could head downstairs to see what was going on. My watch showed it was after one o'clock. When I came out onto the street, I could see a small knot of people along near Maria's taverna. As I approached I could see Maria, Petros and Althaia and a couple of other locals I'd seen around but whom I didn't know. Stavros sat on the steps of the taverna, ranting loudly in Greek, his head in his hands. Maria and the others were trying to quiet him. Althaia spotted me and came to meet me.

"Mr Terry. Sorry that we have woken you."

"What's going on Althaia, what's the matter with Stavros?"

"He drink too much. It is no big problem. It happen some time. He came to Maria to get more Ouzo, he break the door."

"He's so quiet," was all I could think to say.

"He is good man. He has sad story. Sometimes it is too much for him."

"What happened?"

"He lose his wife and daughter, they die in car crash."

"That's horrible. Is there anything I can do?"

"No Mr Terry, we make sure someone is with him until he is sober again. We worry that some time he might try to hurt himself. Maria is sister to his wife. She try to look after him."

"Writer. You come." I switched my gaze from Althaia to Stavros. The big head had lifted. He had spotted me.

"Writer, we feesh." He was waving me over.

I looked at Althaia and she nodded, so I walked over. Stavros tried to stand but fell back onto the step. I sat down beside him.

"Hey my friend, are you okay?"

Stavros smiled at me with blurry eyes.

"We feesh again, you and me."

"Yes, we fish again."

"We drink ouzo. He turned towards Maria. "Get ouzo," he said in English.

"No, no," I said.

"Yes, get ouzo," he yelled again.

Maria stood beside me.

"He will fall asleep soon. Maybe you have ouzo with him inside my house, then he fall asleep there. Is bad if he asleep here. Too hard to carry."

I nodded in understanding.

"Stavros, let's go inside and drink ouzo."

He had started singing in Greek.

"Ney, we drink ouzo."

"Come, let's go inside," I said.

Maria and I helped Stavros to his feet where he swayed like the mast of a schooner in a rolling sea. We moved unsteadily through the taverna into the house behind, where Maria and Petros lived. Stavros fell onto the couch, yelling again for an ouzo bottle. The others had gone home, including Althaia. Petros smiled at me and headed to bed. It was only Maria and me with the gentle giant.

Maria poured two glasses of ouzo, handing them to us.

"Yamas," yelled Stavros.

"Yamas."

Stavros swallowed the glassful in one swig, slamming the glass down on the arm of the lounge where it rocked and then tipped onto the floor without smashing. A switch seemed to flick inside the huge head, his eyes had the thousand-yard stare. He said nothing more. Eventually Stavros' head tipped backwards and big snores started erupting from his throat.

"This is good," said Maria. "Thank you."

"No problem. Glad I could do something. I didn't realise he was your brother-in-law."

Maria smiled and nodded as she understood what I was saying.

"Yes, yes. He is my, what do you call it?"

"Brother-in-law."

"Yes, he is my brother-in-law. He is good man. This does not happen very much." She seemed to be apologising for the big man's behaviour.

"Althaia said that he lost his wife and daughter."

"Yes, my sister and their daughter. They visit family in Thessaloniki. Big truck drives into car. They both die."

Stavros snorted at this point, his head rocking forward and then to the side, toppling him, down onto the couch. Maria lifted his feet up onto the couch and them covered him with a blanket.

"Good, good."

"That is very sad Maria. I am sorry for Stavros and you for losing your sister."

Maria was on the verge of tears. She smiled.

"You are good friend to Stavros for coming to help him. He likes you."

"Well, he made me a Greek fisherman."

She laughed.

"We can sleep now," she said. "He is safe."

She gave me a big hug near the door and I bid her good night and walked back to the hotel.

11

Stan and Errol drove quietly away from the island capital some time after two in the morning.

Stan was driving, in contrast to previous outings. Errol had ignored Eve's orders not to drink. He had reasoned with Stan that his system had not been without a drop of something in it for so long, that he feared it might shut-down without it. Stan warned him about what the woman had said.

"Fuck her, toe-rag bitch. Out at all-hours, taking her abuse. Who does she think she is?"

There wasn't much to choose from at the supermarket. He hated ouzo, and wine was for queers. So that left raki.

"Tastes like shit," he said after the first swallow, before re-filling his glass and downing the contents. He did his best to cajole Stan into drinking with him, accusing him of selling out his sex and less complimentary references regarding his manhood. Eventually Stan gave in. Errol had consumed half the bottle by this stage. They finished the bottle about an hour shy of the time they were supposed to wake and get going after the final piece. When the alarm sounded, Errol was comatose and Stan wasn't exactly feeling sharp.

"Errol, wake up, you bastard. We have to go. Come on, you great arse. The boss'll kill us if the bitch tells him we let her down."

Stan could see no other alternative, he couldn't do the job without Errol. He walked to the fridge and removed the jug of cold water, upending it into Errol's face as he lay snoring on the couch. It had the desired affect. Errol woke coughing and gagging, thinking he'd been water-boarded. He sat up, looked at Stan, and then vomited across the coffee table.

"The FUCK," he yelled, when he had stopped vomiting.

"Quiet! Keep it down. We need to go."

"Fuckin' kill you. Why'd you do that."

"We need to get this done."

Stan helped Errol to his feet and out the front door. They climbed into the van but had not made it out of the driveway before Errol demanded he stop, so he could throw open the door and vomit.

"Fuckin' wog shit," he said wiping his mouth on his sleeve. "Good as gold now. Whattya waitin' for? Let's go."

Errol vomited twice more before they'd driven half way.

"Are you right to do this?" asked Stan before he started driving again.

Errol turned to Stan, his face pale and eyes watering.

"Don't think I can." With that he opened the door and vomited again. It was too much for Stan, the smell permeated the cab. He pushed open his own door and vomited. Stan said nothing further, turning the van around and heading back to their house.

"What'll we tell the bitch."

"We'll have to make something up."

12

Eve's children ensured that she did not get to enjoy a sleep-in. She sat sipping an instant coffee, holding the bracelet in her hand. She should have thrown it away. But for some silly reason she had put it in the drawer of her bedside table where Hannah had found it, thinking it would make a fine pendant for Mr Toukley, her teddy bear.

Eve was in no doubt that Terry knew what it was and must be wondering how it ended up in her room and on the bear. But, short of saying something to her, there was not much he could do about it. She didn't know for certain whether it had even belonged to the boy. It had simply been with the rope on the desk in his room. One more day, she thought. If those idiots did their job last night I should have the last piece. We can get them onto the boat tonight and then I can leave tomorrow.

But only if those fools have done their job.

The men had come courtesy of her associate in London.

She had used the man's services on many occasions, chiefly for getting items into and out of places—something he was very good at—items which she did not want to come to the attention of the UK's, and other countries, customs authorities, nor the various groups and organisations which were trying to stop the smuggling of antiquities around the world.

Eve knew the system well. She knew that many of the relevant authorities in countries like Egypt and several in Central and South America, where the pickings were lucrative and much in demand, were ineffectual and rife with corruption. She rarely felt guilt about moving pieces around the world through her network of collectors, her attitude being that most of the pieces were safer and better looked after than they would be by remaining in their country of origin.

And so her associate in London provided a valuable and reliable service to her. She knew she would not have the bank balance she had—the offshore ones specifically—without him. She had a good relationship with him and was very careful to keep it that way. But, he was a criminal, and she never forgot that.

It was the first time she had required physical assistance to get her work done. It was new territory for her, working with pieces this big and requiring help to do it. And she was beginning to regret it. The reward was substantial but it wouldn't be much good to her if she was locked up inside Holloway Prison, or worse, here in Greece. The idea sent shivers down her spine and made her despise the two dolts even more. She knew it would be their mistake that would bring about such as outcome, not something she might do.

And if there was even the remotest chance that something might go wrong she wouldn't hesitate for a second to abandon the pair of them to the Greek police. They didn't know who she was. She was simply the woman employing them. The men had arrived separately and stayed at the house she had rented in the main town, bringing a hired van from Athens. She had made sure that any time she was with them that she wore sunglasses or some sort of head covering to make sure that they would have difficulty in describing her to anyone else.

And she had an ace up her sleeve. But that was something she would only use as a last resort.

Her fear of incarceration was not simply due to the likelihood of losing her kids. It was as much about her own experience as a child. She had grown up in juvenile facilities, courtesy of a drug addicted mother and a non-existent father. She hadn't seen her mother in twenty years and had no interest in finding her. Eve thought she was most likely dead anyway, from alcoholism or drugs.

Eve had done her time in foster homes and knew that she didn't want her life to go the way of so many others that she knew with this kind of upbringing. She had always known she had a good brain, but more importantly she had a strong work ethic and self-belief. She had put herself through university, working in pubs and restaurants to pay for it. She was beholden to no-one. She had briefly let her guard down when she met and married her ex, the kids coming soon afterwards. She quickly realised that he had tapped into her insecurities and was looking for a meal ticket. That wasn't going to happen.

She waited until she had built up the gallery business before she told him to go. When he threatened her with the courts—it was money he wanted, not the kids—she tossed him an envelope and told him that there was no more. He only came back once. She didn't like owing favours but was happy to have the problem dealt with expeditiously by her London associate. She had asked that her husband be encouraged to stay away but to remain breathing. She knew that this left enough scope for her associate to work within. She had not heard from her husband again.

And now here she was, close to her retirement goal. She had visions of a little gallery in Spain or France or maybe Italy. All above board. Something for her enjoyment. A quaint place where she would raise her kids and send them off to university.

She thought she might even find herself a benefactor. She knew her looks would stand her in good stead for a few more years and a rich suitor would help to top things off nicely. She didn't want to be burdened with another husband. She would be happy to be the other woman, as long as it came with a pay-day somewhere down the track. All within her grasp.

The only thing that frightened her was not achieving it.

13

I slept late. It had taken a while to get to sleep. It wasn't just the late-night Stavros outing, the bracelet issue was now troubling me worse than ever. It wasn't going to go away. I would have to do something about it.

I dressed and went to Maria's for breakfast. She gave me a hug when I walked in and thanked me again for my efforts the previous night.

"Where is he?"

"He wake early and go home. He, what you say, very shy today?"

"Ah, embarrassed. You mean he is troubled by what others think?"

"Yes, embarrass. He do this each time. He say sorry and I not see him for some days. He will come back with octopus to give me tomorrow or next day as gift. I tell you help as well. He say he remember you are there."

"I hope he doesn't leave octopus in my room."

Maria laughed and went off to get my breakfast. I loved the morning yoghurt and fruit. I had stopped eating cooked food in the morning, enjoying the yoghurt with some muesli, and then lingering over a couple of Greek coffees and maybe a small piece of halva if Maria insisted.

However, this morning was not as restful as others as I pondered my bracelet problem. The only way I was going to put this issue to bed was to find out whether the dead boy had worn a bracelet. But, how was I going to do this without making it obvious that I had an interest? It was Althaia who helped solve part of the problem. She came and sat with me to have a morning coffee as she had done on a number of mornings.

"Why are you all dressed up this morning, Althaia, is there another famous writer coming?"

She laughed.

"Mr Terry," she insisted on calling me this even though I had suggested she drop the 'Mr'. "You are cheeky man. No, it is not another writer. It is a sad morning. Today is little Alfio's funeral. The little boy who died in the mountains."

I made a quick decision.

"Would it be a problem or rude if I was to come along with you? Is it a private thing for families and friends?"

"No, is good that you come. Many people will be there. It is nice thing that you go. Many from this village will go as well. I go with Maria and Petros in their car. You come with us. We will leave at ten."

Maria came out with our coffee. Althaia explained my request in Greek to Maria. Maria smiled and looked at me like a favoured son. I drank my coffee and went back to my room to dress in the best outfit I could muster, a pair of jeans, boat shoes and a shirt with buttons. It wasn't exactly formal wear, but it was clean and tidy. It would have to do. I walked back to Maria's.

We all climbed into the tiny car and headed out of town, driving up across the range, turning off the main road onto a narrow road that ran into the small village where Alfio had lived. Maria explained on the drive that they all knew Alfio's mother very well, that she often bought the woman's goat cheese and meat for her restaurant. Althaia added that there would be a wake held after the funeral.

The village was tiny, a plaka, store, church and a few scattered houses all perched on a plateau, surrounded by tall peaks. A massive tree hung over the plaka. It would be a wonderfully cool place to sit on a hot day. And to ensure that the scene was undeniably Greek, an olive grove ran off one side of the plateau, disappearing into one of the valleys below.

Petros parked near the church with the many other vehicles. A large crowd loitered near the steps. The church was tiny and I wondered how we would all fit. It might have been small but it was impressive. It was painted an eye-aching white, the morning sun already pulsating off its walls. It was spotlessly pristine. The bell hung above the blue front door. The facade-like structure of square stepping leading up to the bell, contrasted the rounded blue dome set behind it.

I wasn't remotely religious and had little time, particularly, for the trappings of any form of Christianity. But whether it was the occasion, or something else I didn't understand, this little church seemed somehow to command my respect.

I tagged along behind the three while they talked to friends outside the church. The bell rang soon after and we moved inside. Once we were all settled the priest entered along with the pall-bearers carrying the casket which was laid in front of the altar. The priest looked older than the church. He was tiny and had a long grey beard, the only contrasting colour to his black cassock and hat. He looked like a character from a Tolkien book.

Althaia explained in a whisper that the casket was open, a tradition in their church, and that we would have the opportunity to see Alfio at the end of the service and to put flowers near his casket. The priest lead the congregation through various hymns and prayers.

Only one other person spoke. Althaia explained that it was Alfio's uncle, who also lived in the village. Although I couldn't understand a word of what he said, Alfio's uncle moved me with his quiet dignity and control. The tears flowed freely down his weathered cheeks but he spoke clearly and confidently. I could see many people nodding in agreement with the things he was saying.

When the service concluded, the congregation formed a line to file past the casket, many leaving flowers. I wasn't looking forward to it but thought I needed to do it. He looked very peaceful and comfortable, dressed, no doubt, in his best clothes. He looked so young and defenceless that it made me doubt my suspicions that anyone would want to harm him. But then my heart jolted in my chest. There were two framed photos next to the casket. One, a wide shot of Alfio with his goats. And the second a tight shot of his face with an arm slung around the neck of one of the goats. And there on his wrist, the bracelet. It was identical. I was positive.

I didn't know what to think. It was only a short walk up the hill to the cemetery. Althaia held my arm up the incline, wiping her eyes and blowing her nose several times, but saying little. Several more hymns were sung at the graveside before the casket was lowered into the ground. Maria and Althaia threw flowers into the grave.

"Come," said Maria, as the service ended. "It is time for Makaria. We eat." She laughed "We Greeks can always eat."

I laughed with her.

We walked back to the church and into a small hall off to the side where trestle tables had been set up and piled high with food and drinks. Althaia and Maria made sure I did not go hungry. Each time it looked like I had finished something, another treat would appear.

"Come," said Althaia, "and meet Alfio's mother and sisters."

We stepped our way through the sea of mourners.

Maria touched a woman on the arm, embracing her as she turned. Althaia then repeated the process. They spoke in Greek and then turned towards me.

"Thank you for coming. It is very kind that you respect my son." I was surprised that her English was so good.

"I am very sorry for your loss," was the best I could do.

Most of the mourners were filing out of the church. We gradually made it to the car, stopping to speak with many people on the way, each time I was introduced as the 'famous writer'. The car ride was quiet on the return journey.

"You come later for dinner?" asked Maria when we stopped in the village.

"Where else would I go?"

She smiled.

Althaia and I walked back to the hotel. I decided I needed a swim at the beach to clear my head. I changed into my swimming shorts and a t-shirt, not bothering with footwear, and walked the length of the beach, around the bay, until I reached the rocks at the far end, near the harbour entrance, opposite the break-water where Stavros' boat was moored. Althaia had told me this was the best swimming place. The water was deeper and the fish plentiful. I climbed along up onto a rock platform and walked a little further to where I could see that the water was deep. It was amazingly clear. I dived.

I realised before I hit the water that I was higher up than I realised. I had never been much for diving or swimming, and it was reflected in my entry, thighs slapping on the surface, barely avoiding a full bellyflop. But beyond the appalling entry it was sublime. The water was a little cooler out here where it was deeper. I breast-stroked along the shore line out into the open ocean. It was very liberating if not a little scary. The first thing I thought of was the size of the octopus that Stavros and I had hauled into his boat. I had swum far enough I decided. I about-faced and swam back to the beach.

I dried myself off and climbed back up onto the rocks, to sit and watch the light play out on the water as the sun disappeared behind the hills. It was full dark as I strolled along the sand back towards the village. For no good reason I decided to walk back along the road into the village. I left the beach and walked through the light scrub, hitting the road soon after. I turned towards the village and was almost at the first houses when I saw someone talking through the window of a van. With the village lights behind her, I could see that it was Eve. I froze, not wanting her to see me. Not sure why.

I stepped off the road and approached a little closer through the long grass and scrappy trees, hopeful that a scorpion didn't latch on to my bare feet. Did they even have scorpions in Greece?

I approached as close as I dared. What was I doing? My heart was pounding in my ears. I could hear Eve's voice but could not make out the words. I was too frightened to go any closer, knowing I would give myself away and end up very embarrassed.

But even with this I wondered who she was talking to. She had not given me any indication that she knew anyone on the island. Especially anyone who spoke the kind of English I could hear coming from the van. It wasn't long before the van started, turned and headed away from the village. I could hear Eve's footsteps on the road growing fainter. I waited a couple of minutes and then walked back through the scrub to the beach, not risking her seeing me arrive on the road. Again, I wasn't sure why I was playing James Bond, but something told me I needed to be careful.

I went to my room and put on my sandals and headed to Maria's. What do I do next, I wondered? I knew too much now, not to pursue it. What possible link could Eve have with Alfio? It didn't make any sense. Even though she had the bracelet it didn't mean that she had any role in his death, did it?

And I wasn't sure what my relationship with Eve would be like, following our last meeting.

14

Eve had called the men an hour or so before, as agreed, to confirm they had procured the final piece the previous night. She had warned them repeatedly against saying anything incriminating—after explaining what incriminating meant—on a mobile phone. So Stan had used the agreed code to say that things hadn't gone to plan and they did not have the piece.

Stan broke the connection and looked at Errol.

"Why is it that I seem to end up delivering the bad news to her?"

Errol shrugged.

"She wasn't happy. She wants us to meet her in the usual spot."

The last piece was at some small ruins at a village on the north side of the island. Eve had been there twice by herself to confirm it was what she needed. She had photographed it—as she had done with the other two pieces—and given the picture to Stan and Errol. It was bigger than the other pieces and commensurably heavier, but the distance to carry it much shorter than for the other pieces, only a handful of yards.

The downside was that the ruins were very near the village.

Eve was seething when she arrived at the van.

"What happened?" Her teeth were clenched tight and her fists balled at her sides.

Stan had again drawn the short straw to deliver the rehearsed lie.

"A car started driving up the road towards the ruins when we were getting ready to grab it. We didn't think it was a good idea if they could identify us, so we took off."

"It could have been the police," was Errol's input from the passenger seat.

"Is that right? You pair of useless idiots. You've got one more chance tonight. If it doesn't come out, I'll be making a call to London. And if I do that, you two will need to consider whether you want to go back there. Understand?"

"Yes missus," said Stan.

Eve turned her back and walked off without another word, hoping she had frightened them enough. She decided she would speak to her London contact, whatever the outcome. Should she go now, she wondered as she walked? Should I go with the pieces I've got, get them onto the boat and then get out of this place? It wasn't going smoothly.

But she knew she couldn't go yet. The job wasn't complete and she had her professional reputation to consider, not to mention the likelihood of a substantially reduced reward if she offered only two pieces. No, she had promised three pieces, and three pieces it would be. But this would mean delaying her departure for at least another day. Another night to grab the piece, and then wait a further night to get all three pieces off the island.

The longer it took the greater the chance that someone would discover that that the first two pieces were missing from the ruins. And it wasn't that someone might discover the missing pieces. What would happen now that the writer had seen the bracelet? She was annoyed, not so much about the fact that he'd seen it, rather that she wasn't sure how to deal with it. Feeling like she was not in control was her greatest frustration.

15

The ruins above the port village were the only ones on the island that Sergios Koutsoukis actively disliked. Not because they were less important than the other sites on the island, or that they were somehow less impressive or less attractive. He disliked them because they were the only ones he could not drive to.

Ancient ruins were a mainstay of the island's popularity—like so many of the Greek islands—behind it's beaches and restaurants in importance, a combination that helped to ensure a constant stream of tourists through the high-season months. And the ruins above the port village were arguably the most historically significant, a fact reinforced over many years by scholars from all over the world.

But why were they so hard to get to, Sergios would often grumble. But however annoying it was, Sergios was careful not to complain too loudly. He had held the job of sites superintendent, monitoring the condition of the sites, for over twenty-five years. These kinds of jobs were rare, jobs in the islands that brought in a regular government income. He did not want to give it up any time soon.

It wasn't a difficult job. He merely had to visit the sites and check that everything was in order and report any work that was needed to the local government office. There was never much to report. A bit of pruning or mowing and perhaps the occasional installation of a fence to keep tourists out of more sensitive areas. The ruins above the port required less maintenance than all the others, for the same reason that he hated going there. Because they required more of an effort to get to.

Sergios had two options when it came to reaching the ruins. He could walk from the port village up the hillside and hundreds of steps or he could drive to the end of the road in the mountains and walk from there. He had chosen the latter for many years. While the walk was much longer than the climb from the village, it was over much flatter terrain, an important consideration given his expanding girth and the subsequent pressure on his bad knee.

Why couldn't the government simply extend the road to the ruins. It would be better for everyone. Easier for the tourists, easier for the maintenance men and certainly easier for him. This was the same conversation he had been mumbling to himself for many years, every time he had to make the walk. But today there was something that pushed aside his grumblings the instant he arrived at the site. Something was missing. It was obvious the second he set foot onto the stone dais, one, no two pieces were missing. He was aghast. Nothing like this had ever happened before. He couldn't believe it.

Maybe, he thought, they had been taken for analysis by historians or scientists. But why wouldn't someone tell me. He pulled his mobile from his pocket and called the local government office. No, no permission has been sought or given to remove any pieces, his boss confirmed.

Sergios described the pieces as best he could from memory and then took several photos of the places they had been taken from, the indents in the hard ground showing clearly that something had previously lain there. He sent the photos to the office. Sergios knew that they would be able to quickly establish which pieces were gone, from the photographic files held in the office.

"Sergios, before I call the police and the antiquities protection department in Athens, check the site thoroughly to confirm nothing else is missing," said the office manager.

Sergios walked two full circuits of the site. Satisfied that there was nothing more amiss, he called back to confirm. He also confirmed that he had not seen anyone else around during his visit.

"What about the other sites?" asked Sergios. "We should check them as well and see if anything is missing."

"Yes, you're right. How quickly can you get back here?"

Sergios headed back to his car making his best possible speed, looking like an emperor penguin on the march.

16

There was no sign of Eve when I arrived at Maria's that afternoon. The restaurant was very quiet, only one other table occupied by an older couple. Maria waved from inside the building which housed a few other tables and the kitchen, and soon came out to sit with me, bringing a small carafe of the dry local white that I enjoyed.

I asked whether she had seen Stavros. She laughed and said he had been in that very day with a bucket full of octopus for which he refused payment. Maria explained that he was worried about what I would think of him.

"Should I go and see him?"

"Yes, he will be home. Go to his house. He would be happy if you see him."

Maria explained how to get to his house.

"How is writing?" she asked.

It was a good question and one which I didn't really want to answer. Apart from the one spurt on the travel piece, I hadn't put word one into my laptop. At least for once my excuse wasn't laziness or lack of an idea. The death of Alfio, and the missing bracelet, had absorbed most of my time.

"The writing is ok, Maria. But I really need to do some more."

"You are great writer. It will come for you."

"Thanks Maria."

A little smirk lit up her face.

"And the woman with the children. How is that?"

"Maria," I said in mock severity. "What are you talking about?"

"I see these things. What do you call them. Holiday romancing."

I laughed out loud.

"There is no holiday romancing."

"She is very beautiful," said Maria.

"Yes, she is. But there is no romancing."

A group of four walked in and Maria left me, with my order for the meatballs and red sauce, the meal I had eaten on my first night. And a salad and bread of course. I was getting very predictable.

So what was I going to do with Eve? I had to ask her about the bracelet. She was leaving soon, maybe tomorrow, I couldn't remember. If I didn't act soon she would be gone and I would be left with what-I-should-have-done. The chance to address the issue walked in two minutes later, with her kids. And if I was worried that she may not want to engage, I was mistaken.

Eve made eye contact as soon as she saw me and smiled. I smiled back and waved her over.

"Come and sit with me."

"Thanks," she said, getting the kids seated.

Maria came back shortly afterwards with my salad and meatballs and took Eve's order. We worked our way through the meal discussing nothing in particular, Eve distracted frequently keeping her children focused on finishing their food. The kids begged to be allowed to play on the sand. The tide was out and so she told them they could play down below where we were sitting, in the light from the restaurant.

Eve and I both ordered coffee and halva from a bemused Maria, who gave me a cheeky wink from behind Eve's back. Romancing was the furthest thing from my mind at this point.

"Eve, I need to ask you something a little strange."

She looked at me, her face neutral.

"That bracelet, on Hannah's bear, where did you get it?"

"That's a bit random," she said, her eyes locked on mine. "What do you mean, where did I get it?"

There was nothing for it, I blurted it out. I explained my walks to the ruins and how I had found the bracelet and the piece of rope. And how they had then disappeared from my room. She bridled at this point, but I put my hand up before she could speak and continued, explaining that I had gone to Alfio's funeral and seen the photo of him wearing it.

Eve sat back without responding, arms folded, staring at me. I didn't know what to do. Now that I had said it out loud, I felt like an idiot. It sounded crazy to me. How must it sound to her?

"Look," I said, "it must sound nuts, having just said it out loud, it sounds nuts to me. But I haven't been able to get it out of my head since the bracelet disappeared."

"I'm not sure what you want me to say," said Eve after a long pause. "Are you accusing me of breaking into your room to steal a cheap bracelet?"

"NO, no, I'm not sure what I'm doing. It's just, it just looked like the same bracelet."

"Hannah found the bracelet on the way to the beach. It looked cheap so I never bothered giving it to anyone. She had taken a shine to it. So if I was guilty of anything it was that."

The look on her face scared me, I was on dangerous ground.

"Is it the little boy's bracelet? Did you show it to his mother?"

"No. No, nothing like that."

"So you're not even sure it's his. You found it in a place where thousands of people walk. It could belong to anyone."

"Yes, you're right. I'm sorry, it sounds crazy but I needed to say it. I convinced myself I was nuts but then it disappeared and then I found out Alfio had lost one. Sorry. I hope I haven't insulted you."

"It's okay. I probably should have given the bracelet to Althaia to see if anyone came looking for it. But as I said, it looked cheap, so I didn't worry about it. We're probably both guilty of something." She finished with a smile.

I was relieved.

"Maybe I can borrow it, and check with Alfio's mum. That'll put all my conspiracy thinking to bed, once and for all."

"I would've suggested doing the same thing, but unfortunately Hannah's already lost it. She came crying to me this afternoon saying she couldn't find it. You know kids."

"Ah well, it doesn't really matter," was all I could think to say.

"I'll have a good look for it," she said, looking me in the eye. Eve looked at her watch.

"I'd better get these monsters home to bed. Did you fancy another balcony wine?"

"Yeah, that'd be great."

"Give me forty-five minutes to get them sorted, then come over. I'll leave the door unlocked. Don't bother knocking."

She gathered her brood and headed off. I watched her go, not sure how I felt. I was happy to get my thoughts off my chest. And I was very happy that Eve was still talking to me. But for some reason I still didn't feel satisfied with the outcome. What did I want, what was I expecting? Eve to confess to some heinous crime? I couldn't believe she was still speaking to me with what I had thrown at her, let alone inviting me for a drink. And then I remembered her conversation with someone in a van on the edge of the village. I still had more questions than answers.

I walked inside and paid Maria for my meal. She smiled at me and didn't say anything.

"Maria, stop it. I thought you Greek women were supposed to be shy and respectful."

She laughed.

"You write romance in books. Time to live it."

I walked off, shaking my head. I turned the corner and headed up the dark, narrow, cobbled street following the directions Maria had given me to get to Stavros' place. I walked across the plaka, past Voula's restaurant and down a small street running behind the plaka. I smiled when I saw Stavros' house. It was like his boat: small, neat, tidy and freshly painted. Even the colours were the same.

He beamed when he saw me.

"Writer. You are here. Please to come in." He stepped back from the doorway.

His house was as neat inside as out. A huge chair—undoubtedly his chair—was the centre piece of his front room.

"Come, come, you sit." He waggled his fingers in the direction of his chair.

"No, this is your chair."

"No, no, is good, you sit, please."

I did as I was bid, feeling like I might disappear inside the floral behemoth. He took great pleasure in pulling the lever on the side of the chair, my feet shooting up into the air. He smiled, seemingly content that I was comfortable. He left the room and I could hear the clink of glasses nearby. He came back with a bottle and glasses on a big silver tray.

"We have some Ouzo," he said pouring the oily fluid into the small glasses. He paused halfway through the first one and looked at me, "but not so much."

"No," I said. "Too much is not so good."

He looked at my face, seemingly for any hint of mirth.

"Cheers," he said.

I laughed.

"Yamas."

We talked in our limited fashion about his recent fishing exploits. He explained how he was having trouble with the engine on his boat, but had sorted the problem. Catches had not been as good as the day that I went along, but okay. There was no mention of his drunken night or my role in it.

"You come feesh again soon."

"I would like that. Now, I must go. I have someone else to visit."

He nodded his big head. Probably thinking the same as me, that we had exhausted our conversation topics. He clapped me on the shoulder as we stood at the front of his house and said thank you, before turning and walking back inside. I wasn't sure what the thank-you was for, but I was happy that Stavros seemed to be happy.

I walked back to the hotel, quietly opening the door to Eve's room without knocking, as she had suggested. I couldn't see her, but I could hear her speaking to someone, and she didn't sound happy.

17

Eve waited until both kids were asleep, which didn't take long, before she removed the bracelet from Mr Toukley. She held it up in front of her eyes, and shook her head.

"You, my cheap friend, are causing me some issues." She dropped it into her bag, thinking she would drop it into the harbour the next day. And then, she thought, one more night and I can be out of here, but only if those two dolts do their jobs.

And then her phone rang.

Stan didn't fall for it this time. When Errol tossed him the phone, he tossed it back.

"No, not this time. You do it. You're the bloody reason we're in trouble."

Errol didn't know what annoyed him more, Stan not doing what he wanted, or Stan figuring him out.

Errol didn't mind Stan, as far as it went. That was about as expansive as Errol got about anybody. Errol's life, ironically, was not that different to Eve's. But they had played the shitty hands they had been dealt very differently.

Like Eve, Errol had grown up in a series of foster homes, after the final beating his father had given him, at age eleven, had put him into hospital with busted rubs, a broken arm and two black eyes. It hadn't improved much after that. He'd followed a series of bad role models and soon found himself in various juvenile detention facilities.

He was released from his final stay on his eighteenth birthday. He celebrated by tracking down his father, greeting him in the hallway of his seedy council flat with a baseball bat. Errol's only conclusion from all this was the realisation that the only person he could rely on in this world was himself, the one trait that he and Eve shared.

He pushed the pre-set button to call Eve and put the phone on speaker. He wasn't expecting a warm response.

"Why are YOU calling me?"

"Look, we went for a drive past, earlier, to have a look and there were cops there. Lots of people taking photos and looking around. Something is going on and we're not sure if we should go back. It's easy to see someone approaching from a long way off, and we'll be sitting ducks late at night."

Eve took a big breath before responding.

"You'll only be sitting ducks, as you so eloquently put it, if you say something stupid if someone stops you. Just do what you're being paid to do. Don't make me call your boss. Go for a drive past at two am and see if there's anyone around, if there's not, get it done. If there's people there, don't stop."

"Yeah, that's easy for you to say," said Errol, his temper getting the better of his good sense. "But it's a long road in. The only way we can know if someone is there is to drive in, and once we're on that road we have to drive to the place to turn around. It'll look bloody suspicious if someone's there watching."

Before Eve could say anything, Errol continued, his confidence buoyed by Eve's lack of a response.

"What if they know about the other stuff? What if they're checking other places? Because that's what it looked like. And what if they're stakin' these places out? Why don't we take the stuff we've got and get out. Me and Stan don't want to be doing time in a wog prison."

He paused before going on.

"And we don't want to have to be answering questions about anyone else being involved, do we?"

Stan winced in the background and shook his head.

"Are you threatening me? You have the gall, you piece of trash, to threaten me? You had a simple job to do and you've messed it up at every turn. We can't go, as you suggest, because the task isn't done, and that's because you've not completed it. Now you have a choice," Eve continued, teeth clenched. "You can climb in your little white van, and drive past the site, at the appropriate time, or I can call your boss right now and explain to him why his high-priced help is not doing the job they're being paid to do. Which will it be? Hurry up and decide."

Errol wasn't sure what to say. He looked at Stan, who looked down at the floor. Four or five seconds passed with nothing being said.

"Look missus, we don't need to involve the boss." Errol's voice didn't quite have the force of his previous statement. "But you need to trust us." It was almost pleading. "It won't help any of us if we get caught. Let's leave it another night. We can go and have another look tomorrow. And see if there's anything happening. If it's quiet, we can do it tomorrow night, right as rain." Stan nodded to Errol in agreement.

There was another pause in the conversation. Eve knew she was snookered. She couldn't force them to do it and as much as she hated to admit it to herself, the big idiot might be right. She wasn't unaware of the Greek government's harsh view towards people who stole antiquities.

"One more night," was all she said, delivered with all the venom she could muster, before breaking the connection.

I backed quietly out of the room, closing the door carefully, and then tip-toed back along the hallway to my own room, opening the door and going inside. I'd forgotten to breath for ten seconds or so and let out a long breath.

"What the fuck is going on?" I asked out loud.

Eve was walking into the lounge room as she finished the conversation and heard the door click shut.

"Shit," was all she said.

I wasn't sure what to do. I wasn't sure what I had heard. She was up to something. It must involve whomever she was talking to in the van. She wasn't happy, something wasn't working out for her. But I still didn't know anything. She could have been speaking to someone anywhere in the world. All I know is they're doing something at two o'clock in the morning. It could be anywhere.

It was like the bracelet issue. I was going off half-cocked. I didn't know enough to make any sense of it. And I certainly didn't want to confront her again, only to end up feeling like a bigger dick than last time. I had to get back to her room. She was expecting me.

I took a big breath and pulled my door shut behind me. I opened the door to Eve's room and stepped inside. She was standing in the middle of the room with her arms folded, looking concerned.

18

By the time Sergios arrived back at the government office in the island's capital there were many more vehicles parked out the front than he was used to seeing, police cars among them. But it didn't surprise him. The theft and illegal sale of antiquities had always been a big problem in Greece, and had become much worse since the country's economic woes had escalated. There was money to be made, and he had been asked on more than a few occasions if he was interested in making a bit extra.

Sergios had shut these offers down quickly and had even reported a couple of contacts to the police. It wasn't only about his job security. It was much more than that. He was a proud islander. He had told anyone who would listen that the ruins and the artefacts belonged to all Greeks and no-one had the right to profit from them. These people were stealing the identity of the Hellenic people, he liked to say.

And he knew it wasn't something being perpetrated solely by criminal gangs. He had seen farmers buying metal detectors and knew what they were up to. Looking for coins and other small metal objects which were easy to move and sell, especially during the tourist season. He knew that the department charged with policing the theft of antiquities was woefully under-resourced, so he saw it as his duty to play his part. He didn't feel good about reporting people, especially those he knew, and on more than a few occasions had warned people, giving them a chance to curb their ways. But, once they had been warned, Sergios gave no second chances.

He walked into the office, which was crowded, mostly with people in various government roles on the island, most of whom he knew.

"Ah, Sergios is here," said his supervisor. "Please, take use through what happened."

Sergios explained what he had discovered.

Led by the island's senior police officer, Captain Ioannis Danellis, the group worked quickly to divide themselves into teams to check the other four sites on the island, which they would do before sunset and then meet back to discuss findings and look at forming watch teams over the next few nights. The office of Antiquities and Cultural Heritage had been informed and someone from that office would be with them the next day.

When they met back at the office a couple of hours later, it was confirmed that nothing else was amiss at the other sites. It was agreed that the teams would drive patrols past the sites over the next two nights to make sure that no other robberies could take place. There was no airport on the island, so monitoring air traffic was not an issue. And there was only one ferry link that carried vehicles. Given the size of the missing pieces, it was agreed that if they were being moved by ferry it would have to be in a vehicle, so they would monitor ferry departures.

Of course, the group acknowledged that the pieces could have been stolen many days earlier and already have been taken off the island. That was the task for the next day, to try and establish when the pieces were last sighted. This would be a job for the police, focusing on the port village, the starting point for the most popular way to access the site.

Other scenarios were also discussed. The pieces could have been, or maybe were going to be, removed by a privately owned boat. The Greek coast guard would be contacted to see if they could spare a patrol boat to monitor boat traffic around the island for a few days. The group agreed that this only left the alternative that the pieces might be hidden on the island to be moved at a later date.

Sergios left the meeting. Heartened by the well-organised response planning, but sad that it was necessary.

19

"Are you okay?" I asked, when I saw the look on Eve's face.

"Yes, yes, sorry, yes, just work issues. Come and have a drink, I need one."

We moved on to the balcony, Eve poured two glasses.

"Cheers," she said, taking a long drink.

"Cheers. So what's up?"

"I had to have some unpleasant words with this idiot who does work for me in Egypt. It's a long story, but I've already paid for a piece, had it cleared through the antiquities authorities, I have all the necessary permits to move it. And this fool, who's supposed to be moving it for me, is worried someone is trying to steal it. So instead of keeping an eye on it. He calls me to tell me he's worried."

I watched her face, it all sounded very plausible and fitted in with the conversation I had overheard.

"Stolen antiquities is a big problem around the world, particularly in countries like this one and Egypt. There's a lot of money to be made. It makes me sick. There are so many people out there with money who claim to have a passion for antiquities and yet so few of them will ask where a piece may have come from, or, more importantly, how it got to them. It's the job of dealers, like me, to help police this. The problem is that there are a lot of shady dealers as well. It makes me sad. It's another great example of the wealthy making their own rules."

It was a passionate speech. I was thankful I hadn't put my foot into it again by asking about the phone call.

"But enough about my problems, let's enjoy our wine," she said raising her glass again.

"So what are your plans?" I asked.

"I think we'll stay a couple more nights and then I'll need to get back to London. Things are mounting up in the office. I'd love to stay longer. What are your plans?"

"I've got another ten days or so. I really need to get some work done. I came to rekindle my writing mojo, but I haven't given it much of a chance."

"Well, you'll always have somewhere to live here if things don't work out. They all seem to love you."

I laughed.

"Fans are fickle creatures. If there's no new book, I think I'd find, even here, that their love for me would wear thin fairly quickly."

"Well, if you're ever passing through London, look me up."

"I'd love to do that. I'd like to see your gallery and see you at work. I saw a brief glimpse of your passion in the museum."

"Yes, well, we all need a passion. You've got yours and I have mine."

"Cheers to that," I said.

20

Sergios had been paired with a young police-woman, Anna Pappas. Sergios lived on the north coast of the island in a small village which was home to one of the sites the group were monitoring. Theirs was an easier job during the night, with the ruins situated on the edge of the village. The road to the ruins started in the village and there was no other way to drive there.

The distance to the ruins was not great but given the terrain, the road meandered around the ridge-line of the hills. From the village it was much quicker to walk, a few hundred metres. Of course Sergios rarely walked there when he did his checks, especially as he was paid mileage rates to use his own vehicle.

Sergios had suggested to Anna that they base themselves at his house for the night. They could take it in turn monitoring the site from Sergios' kitchen which looked directly up to the site. Sergios knew that the only pieces that could be removed were large and heavy, bigger than the missing pieces at the other site. They would need a vehicle to remove them. Therefore they focused on watching the road. And Anna had come prepared with a large pair of binoculars.

Nikoleta, Sergios' wife, fussed around the pair making sure they were well fed. She was proud of her husband and his work to support the island's heritage.

It was a long night for all the groups, who met at the office the next morning. There was nothing to report. Captain Danellis ordered three of his officers to go immediately to the port village to speak with the locals and tourists to see who might have been to the ruins and to try and ascertain when the missing pieces were last sighted. Sergios asked if he might go along, saying that his sister was a hotel owner in the village and would be a useful contact.

When they arrived, Sergios suggested he and Anna head straight for the *Cycladaen*, to talk to his sister. The other pair went off to speak with other hotel owners.

"Althaia is at Maria's having coffee with the writer," said the young woman Althaia paid to help her with cleaning.

"Sergios, what are you doing here?" said Althaia, when she saw him walk in. When Althaia realised that there was a police officer with him she became very concerned, and stood up.

"What is the problem? Is it Rania?" Rania was their elder sister who lived in the capital.

Sergios put both his hands up.

"No, no. It's not Rania, calm down, sit down. It's about some stolen pieces from the ruins above the village."

Althaia sat back down in her chair beside Maria.

"Hello Maria," said Sergios, who had known Maria his whole life.

Althaia switched to English.

"Mr Terry, this is my brother, Sergios."

"Sergios this is Terry, the famous writer I told you about."

Sergios held out his hand.

"And this is Anna," Sergios said in Greek, introducing the young

97

police officer. Sergios rarely spoke English. He turned back to Althaia and Maria.

"Two large pieces have been taken from the ruins. We are trying to find out when was the last time that anyone saw them."

When Althaia explained to Terry what her brother had said, he almost fell off his chair.

Althaia, concern on her face, asked if I was okay.

I didn't know what to say, where to begin, or whether to begin at all.

"No, I'm fine, it's nothing," I said. I needed some time to think about what I knew.

She watched me for a few seconds and then turned back to her brother. Althaia and Sergio had a long conversation in Greek. She turned to me.

"Mr Terry, the police and my brother try to see when the pieces are stolen. Did you take any photos when you go to the site?"

"No, I didn't take my camera with me."

"Did you happen to notice whether it looked like anything had been removed?" It was the young policewoman, Anna, who asked, in very clear English. "I mean did you see any holes in the ground where something was lying?"

"No, no, I don't recall anything like that. But I wasn't really looking either. I probably looked more at the view than the ruins, if you know what I mean."

"Yes, yes, thank you," she said. She turned to Sergios and spoke in Greek.

"Thank you again," she said, turning to me with a smile. "We must go now and talk to others."

Althaia went with them, back to her hotel to assist them to speak with her few other guests, which included Eve. I sat there alone, Maria having gone about her morning routines in the kitchen, which included bringing me a second coffee.

My head was hurting. There were too many details. Like before, I felt like I was going in circles. Every time I had thought I was on to something there was always a good reason why I was wrong. The common denominator was Eve. I could've said something to the policewoman but I was frightened. What would Eve think of me if I sent the police to her door demanding answers to questions she would know could only have come from me?

But what if I was right? What if she was involved? She had a gallery, for god's sake, it was a neat fit. It was too much of a coincidence. But so what? Why wouldn't a dealer in antiquities come to somewhere like Greece for a holiday? It made perfect sense. But then there's the bracelet and the two guys in the van.

Shit, I had to say something to someone. I didn't want to tell Althaia. It would start hares running. The young Greek policewoman, her English was great. I jumped up and walked off to find her.

Eve's heart skipped a beat when she opened the door to see Althaia standing there with a policewoman behind her. But she saw that Althaia was smiling. Althaia explained about the missing pieces and what was going on and introduced Anna.

"That is terrible news. Yes, I visited the ruins when I first arrived, I have some pictures on my mobile phone."

In fact Eve had lots of pictures on her mobile including ones of the missing pieces. She had taken many photos, for future reference, in case there was ever anything else she needed. She wasn't concerned about having photos of the missing pieces. They sat in among all the others without showing an obvious interest.

"This is very good, thank you," said Maria. "Can you please send them to me, this one and this one," said Maria nominating two pictures, clearly showing the missing pieces.

"Happy to do that."

Eve had a thought, she decided it was worth the risk.

"There's an Australian man in the hotel, a couple of doors along, I know he has been to the site as well," Eve looked at Althaia.

"Yes, we have already spoken to him but he did not have any pictures. Thank you again. We must keep going."

When they left her room, Eve drew a long breath and sat down. So he didn't say anything, she thought. But what do I do? It was getting dangerous, with the police involved, but those fools had confirmed there was no activity at the site. Maybe it was time to play her ace. She was hoping she could avoid it. It meant bringing in another player, someone she didn't know, on the say-so of her London associate. She trusted her associate fractionally more than she trusted anyone. Not that much.

It was a relationship based on the best possible thing, profit. It was a black and white arrangement. The kind of arrangement that Eve understood. There was no emotion involved.

She was an attractive woman and knew the effect she had on men and had used this from time-to-time to her advantage in her business dealings. More than a few clients over the years had looked to establish dealings beyond the business kind. But when it came to her relationship with her London associate she played it straight. It was the closest she came to respect. He did his job and did it well, and she made money for them both.

So, her concern about bringing in another player wasn't about trust. It was much simpler than that. It would cost her money. And she would always avoid that where possible. But she realised that the level of risk had increased, to a point where she wasn't comfortable. So it was time for some insurance.

The number was already programmed into her phone.

"Hello," she said when the Greek voice answered. "I understand that we have a mutual friend in London."

21

"How many times should we go past today, you reckon?" asked Stan.

"One," Errol snapped. He was not in good humour. Being cooped up the house was getting to him, as was an extended period without booze. He had not touched another drop since the issue a couple of nights before, concerned that Eve would call the boss.

The boss treated them well enough, but Errol had been around people like him his whole life and knew that this favour only extended as far as it suited. If they cocked up they wouldn't be looking to him for support, not when he was making money out of the woman. They'd be on their own. And if they got back to London there'd no doubt be a visit from some of the other boys, the boys who looked after the boss. His inner circle. And that wouldn't be pretty.

So Errol had stayed off the booze and was treading carefully. But not happily.

"We've been there too many times already, if anyone's watching they'll notice us coming back again and again. No, once this afternoon and then we'll get it done tonight and get the fuck out of this dump."

"Amen to that," said Stan. He'd had enough of Errol's bad humour, but would put up with it for another day. He'd worked with him many times and had figured the best way to deal with his moods was to ignore him. But only up to a point.

Stan was starting to feel it as well. The issue with the boy was eating at him. He'd only tried to discuss it once with Errol, but was left in no doubt about Errol's lack of interest. While they hadn't physically killed him, Stan knew it was their fault. The poor little bugger had taken off through the scrub like a madman and no doubt run straight off a cliff. Stan struggled to get the image out his head. He wasn't sleeping well and was hoping things would settle when the job was done and he was home again.

Stan thought about his own little bloke. He didn't get to see him often but he visited when he could. His ex was fairly reasonable about it, and he didn't mind her new bloke. He was a bit of a toff but didn't speak down to him and welcomed him into their nice digs. Stan knew the kid was better off without him. And that hurt a bit, but he'd make sure he stayed around so he could spend some time with him. He would have a pocket-full of cash after this effort and would be able to buy him something nice. This cheered him.

They climbed into the van just after three in the afternoon and did the short drive to the village on the north coast.

"I reckon I could live somewhere like this," said Stan as they topped the final rise and the village lay below them, the few houses and hotels hugging the tiny bay.

"You'd go fucking mad," said Errol. "One week and I'd be off my rocker. Fuck all to do, and no one to talk to. I'd end up killing some bastard."

"Nah, not me," said Stan. "The quiet life. A bit of fishing. Getting to know the locals. I reckon I could handle that."

"Bollocks," was Errol's considered opinion.

Errol drove down into the village, taking the left onto the road to the ruins. All looked quiet. They could see a group of four heading along the walking track from the village.

"Tourists," said Stan.

"Looks like it."

They drove the winding road to the ruins, the tourists there ahead of them. There were no other vehicles in the parking area as they pulled in.

"We'd better stop and have a look around," said Stan. "Might look a bit odd if we drive off."

Errol parked and they wandered over to the ruins, which sat slightly above the village and had a commanding view of the ocean.

"Fuckin' pile of rocks," was Errol's view of archaeological history.

"You should read some of the signs, it's interesting. Mightn't hurt you to learn something."

"Fuck off, what's the point. I can't believe some rich prick would pay thousands for a piece of useless fuckin' rock."

Stan rolled his eyes but didn't say anything more. They did a quick circuit and climbed back into their van and drove off.

"Well, tonight it is," said Stan.

"Call the bitch and tell her we're on."

Stan pushed Eve's number, it only rang once before she answered.

"Missus, we're looking fine for tonight. Yep, we'll send you a text when we get it done. And then we'll call tomorrow at nine to sort out the departure arrangements."

"Done," said Stan, breaking the connection.

"Well aren't you just the fuckin' bitch's bitch."

"Whatever you say Errol, whatever you say. Let's get some lunch in the village."

22

"Excuse me," I said to the policewoman. She and the man I had met earlier, Althaia's brother, were standing on the corner of the street talking to two other policemen.

She turned towards me.

"Yes?"

"Can I please have a word with you...alone?"

"Okay." She turned to the others and they went off, no doubt to speak to others in the village.

"Is there something you need?"

"There's some things I need to say."

"Okay," she said, a slight hesitation in her voice.

"Can we meet in my room? I would prefer it if no-one sees us talking."

Her brows furrowed and she stared into my face for a few seconds before responding. She must have seen something there.

"Okay, you go now. I will follow in a few minutes."

"I'll leave the door unlocked, don't knock."

I gave her my room number and then headed off. I was sure this was the right thing to do. I needed to talk to someone other than Eve. Anna walked in a few minutes later.

"This is all very mysterious," she said.

I invited her to sit on my bed and then blurted everything out, almost from the minute I had set foot on the island. I explained about the bracelet and the death of poor Alfio. I told her about Eve's gallery in London and her meeting with someone in a white van. And I told her of Eve's explanation each time I raised any issues with her.

Anna let me speak, saying nothing, scribbling furiously in her small note pad. When I had finished I saw uncertainty on her face.

"I have already spoken to this woman, this Eve. She had many photos from the site. Including the missing pieces. What you tell me is very interesting but it is, how do you say it, circumstantial. There seems to be many things that point in certain directions, but nothing concrete, no facts."

"I'm sorry," I said. "I know what you mean, and I'm probably wrong about everything. But I needed to tell someone."

"No, no, it is important. And it will need to be followed up. But I think I will have to be careful and speak with my Captain about it. We must be careful with the tourists. We are told all the time. Tourism is the lifeblood of the island, they tell us," She rolled her eyes as she said this last part. "Sometimes it interferes in how we do our job." She smiled, showing me her perfect teeth. "I had better go now."

I walked her to the door.

"Althaia tells me you are a famous author."

"Well, not all that famous."

She smiled again and walked down the corridor. I watched her go. Watching her go was a pleasant experience, she was very pretty. Whether it was the fact that I had unloaded my concerns or spent time in the company of a beautiful woman, I felt better. There was nothing more I could do now. I shut the door, sat at my desk and opened my laptop. Maybe now I could get some writing done. The worries now belonged to others.

Eve waited until the policewoman walked down the stairs and Terry had closed his door before shutting her own. She had been about to go to the shop and buy some water when she opened her door and saw the policewoman talking to Terry in the hallway, their backs to her. She had pulled her door almost closed and watched them.

What was he up to now? Just when I thought he wouldn't be a problem.

23

The group met back in the government offices of the capital in the early afternoon. The only new addition was the woman from the antiquities protection office in Athens who had arrived on the ferry an hour or so before.

Anna ran through what they had discovered, speaking with the tourists and residents from the port village. She made no mention of her meeting with Terry. Thinking she would raise it with her boss afterwards.

It was Eve's pictures that provided the most recent date on which the missing pieces had been sighted. They had spoken with several other tourists who had been to the site after this, but none were able to recall the pieces or had photos of them.

"Given that the last time we know the pieces were still at the site was many days ago," said Captain Danellis, "I think there is very little point in bothering with any further patrols of the other sites."

The woman from Athens discussed what was the most likely scenario and agreed that the pieces were probably taken from the island many days before.

"The best thing we can do is to check the manifest of the car ferry to see what vehicles have left the island since that time. I will contact Athens immediately and put this into action."

The meeting broke up. Anna approached the Captain and asked to speak to him in private.

"What is it Anna?"

Ioannis Danellis had been a policeman his whole working life. He wasn't a local but had been on the island for almost twenty years. In the eyes of the other residents he might soon qualify as a local. Anna liked working for him. He treated her as he did the men under his charge, something that Anna had found a rarity in Greek policing.

But he also had a temper and could sometimes be frightening. She found his height and beetled brow very intimidating whenever he towered over her making a strong point. But overall she knew she was gaining valuable experience from his sharp intellect. They walked outside and along the footpath away from anyone else.

Anna explained what Terry had told her. She pulled out her notebook ensuring she gave the Captain a full and accurate account of what she had been told by the writer, about the woman from London. She knew he appreciated brevity and accuracy. 'More speed, less haste', was one of his favourite maxims.

He said nothing immediately. She knew he would be ruminating on what she had said and didn't make the mistake of saying anything further until he had responded. She had only made this mistake once before.

"Who else have you discussed this with?"

"No-one."

"You did the right thing." He smiled at his charge. She showed great promise, he thought. It was a shame she was a woman. As a man she could go far in the police service. As a woman her options were more limited. He didn't agree with the way things worked in the service, but was pragmatic about it. Change happened slowly in Greece.

"You show good judgement. As you know we must be very careful with the tourists on our island. Leave this with me. I'll decide what to do with what you've told me. And Anna," he looked into her eyes, "please do not speak to anyone else about this."

"Of course Captain."

24

I had busied myself on my laptop for an hour or so, fiddling with a few ideas but getting nowhere in particular, when a knock on the door interrupted me.

"It is me writer, Stavros."

I smiled and opened the door.

"Kalimera, my friend."

"Come, we drink coffee and a little ouzo."

I didn't need much convincing. I grabbed my wallet and key and pulled the door closed, following the big man down the stairs to Maria's. It was late afternoon and the taverna was empty save for Maria and Petros sitting at their usual table. Maria gave me a hug and Petros shook my hand.

"Sit, sit," said Maria. "I will get you coffee and a LITTLE ouzo," she said smiling at the big fisherman. Stavros said nothing, but his discomfort was obvious.

Petros smiled and said nothing until he spoke to Stavros in Greek. He had still made no attempt to talk to me in English. Maria had said that he could speak some English but was too embarrassed to try in front of me. Althaia arrived a few minutes later and we enjoyed the late afternoon quiet together.

"My brother say that they not find out anything about the robbery, talking to people in the village," she said this in English for my bene-fit.

"Has it happened before, stealing from the ruins?" I asked.

"Some people from the island try to sell some small things they find, to tourists. Coins and small things like that. But nothing so big," said Maria.

"It's very sad."

"Yes," said Althaia. "It is important that they stop this people from doing this. These things they belong on this island and to all Greek people. It is important that they are here. It is important for tourists and important for all Greeks."

I felt guilty that I had other information that I had not shared with them. But I knew it would spread like wild fire around the village, and probably the island if I told them. And deep down I thought they would be angry that I had not told them earlier. No, it was better that I had only told the policewoman.

"Your beautiful friend goes home tomorrow," said Maria, looking me in the eye, a grin on her face.

"Yes, Miss Eve, she goes tomorrow. It is nice to have her here. She is a nice woman," said Althaia, also looking at me.

"You two are as bad as each other," I laughed as I said it. "I didn't come here to meet a beautiful woman, I came here to work."

"Ah, a bit of romancing will be helpful."

"Maria," I said with feigned indignation, "there will be no holiday romancing."

"So when will your next book be ready, when can I read it?" Althaia asked hopefully.

"Althaia, when it is done, you will be one of the first to know."

Althaia beamed and touched my hand across the table.

"I need to make a telephone call," I said. "Is there a pay phone around somewhere." I was keen to check in with the Anna, the pretty policewoman, and to let her know that Eve was leaving tomorrow. I wondered if she knew.

"Where will you ring, to Australia?" asked Althaia.

"No, it is here, on the island."

She pushed her mobile across the table to me.

"Use this."

"Are you sure? I can pay you."

Althaia laughed at me.

"I put big charge on your bill. I joke, local is very cheap," she said, pushing the mobile further towards me with her finger tips.

"Thanks." I picked up the mobile and walked out of the taverna and down towards the jetty, making sure that there was no-one around to hear me. I had Anna's number in my wallet.

"Hello," I said in response to her greeting, "it's Terry…the Australian in the port village."

"Yes, yes. Hello."

"Sorry to bother you, I was wondering how you were getting on with what I had told you. And I wondered if you knew," I looked around again to make sure there was no-one nearby, "that Eve, the woman I talked to you about, was leaving tomorrow."

"No, I did not know this. Thank you for telling me. I have spoken to my Captain about all you have told me. But I will let him know this as well. It is good that you call me."

"How is the investigation going?"

"I cannot say much to you about this." She laughed as she said it. "And there is not much to say. We have not made big progress. But thank you again for the information about this woman. I will pass it on. Please call again, if you think of anything more."

"Okay, thanks. I'll speak to you later."

As soon as I said this I thought how lame it must have sounded to someone who didn't understand the way Australians speak. It was a strange statement when you thought about it. Suggesting to an almost-total stranger that you would speak to them again. It must've sounded bizarre to a young Greek woman.

I walked back to the taverna. A couple of tables now had customers, one of which was occupied by Eve and her children. I saw her look my way as I entered. I gave a small wave and sat down with Stavros and Althaia. Maria and Petros had gone to begin their evening's work.

"Thanks Althaia," I said handing the phone back.

"You go now," said Stavros. It wasn't a question, he gestured towards Eve's table, a hint of a smile threatening to break out under the huge moustache.

"Not you too," I said rolling my eyes.

"I go now," he said rising. He offered me his hand. "Maybe we feesh in two days."

"That sounds great. I would like that."

He turned and walked away, ducking under the awning before stepping into the street.

"I must go as well," said Althaia, leaving me alone at the table. I wasn't sure what to do. I suddenly felt very guilty about what I had told Anna. I didn't regret doing it, but I was scared that if I sat with Eve she would see it in my face. But I thought that if I ignored her, that would be as much a sign of guilt.

Eve made it easy for me.

"Are you coming to sit with us?"

Eve had walked up to my table.

"Hey," I said, a little startled. "Sorry, I was away with the fairies. Yes, absolutely. I was about to come over."

I walked across and sat down. Eve wasted no time in touching the issue that was on my mind.

"The village is certainly buzzing about those stolen pieces from the site. I had a police officer come to my room to speak with me. Did they talk to you? I mentioned that you had been to the site as well."

"Yes, I spoke to her. Here in the taverna."

Eve looked me in the eye.

"I saw her outside your room. Did she forget something?"

"Ah, no ... ah, I, it's ... she asked if I had any photos from the site." It had taken me a while to get it out. I'm sure I was blushing.

"And did you have any?"

"No, I didn't take any. Did you have any?" I knew that she did, Anna had mentioned it, but I thought, in the interests of regaining some composure I should add this.

"Yes, I had lots of pictures. I sent her a couple."

"That's good. That must've been of some help to them. I really didn't have anything useful to tell them."

"Is that right?"

"You're leaving tomorrow?" I thought this might be safer ground.

"Yes, who's giving away secrets?" she said, but with a smile.

"Althaia said you were going."

"Yes, I need to get back to it, as much as I would like to stay longer."

"What time do you go?"

"I'm on the evening ferry."

"I'd like to come and say good-bye if that's okay. And I can help you with your luggage."

"Thank you. That would be nice on both counts."

Maria had arrived with the meals for Eve and the children.

"I'll leave you to it. I want to go and do some more work."

"Not eating?"

"Maybe later. I'll see you tomorrow." I said, rising.

"Okay," was all she said.

I walked back to my room, thinking again about the various snatches of information I had involving Eve. The artefacts were already gone when I overheard her on her mobile berating someone for not doing their job. It could not have had anything to do with them. And given I was carrying her suitcase to the ferry, I would have a fair idea if she was smuggling them off the island. Not that they would go close to fitting in a suitcase.

No, I had stuffed up. But still it kept nagging at me. Like Dan Brown's character, Langdon, in *The Da Vinci Code*, coincidence was a concept I did not entirely trust. But I wasn't sure why I wanted to see her off. It was unlikely I would ever see her again. Was it a form of closure? I wasn't sure. Anyway, it wasn't a big deal.

Eve sat and churned things over in her mind, while her kids finished their desserts.

It was obvious that he was uncomfortable, she thought. Something wasn't right. She trusted her instincts. They had got her to where she was today. Other than hard fact, she relied on little else. But what could he do?

He still didn't know anything, she knew that. And she had played her security card. It would cost her and she would, no doubt, regret the expense when she was back in London, looking at her offshore accounts. But for now she knew it had been the right thing to do. She would be happy when she was on that ferry, the pieces on their way. But, of course, that would depend on the dolts, doing their job tonight and tomorrow.

She hadn't told them that the police knew about the missing pieces. They might know, she thought. But she wouldn't bother telling them. It wouldn't help them. It could only be counter-productive. She didn't want them getting cold feet. It was out of her hands now, and she didn't like that. It provided distance between her and the crime but that, as far as Eve was concerned, was more bad than good. Leaving her fate in the hands of others was not something she enjoyed.

She wouldn't rest comfortably until she had the pieces in the London warehouse. And then she would pack them for movement to the States where they would be received by a grateful and generous client.

25

Stan was nervous. And he sensed that Errol felt the same. They were both on edge, it was that their edges manifested differently. Stan was quiet and contemplative. Errol stormed around looking for fault in everyone and everything. Cursing was frequent.

It should be straight forward enough, thought Stan. Grab one piece, throw it into the van. Bring it back and get a couple of hours kip and then get all three pieces into the van and to the harbour. Easy peasy, lemon squeezy.

Then why did he feel this way? He knew why. It was the issue with the kid. He knew already it was going to stay with him. Getting out of Greece was not going to help.

Alfio was his name. He had seen a picture in a local newspaper and even though it was in Greek, he knew it was the kid. He was standing with some goats with a big smile on his face. There was another photo of people outside a church, the funeral, he figured. He asked the woman in the shop about it. She told him the boy's name and explained that he wasn't right in the head. And that it was very sad, sad for his mother, who the woman in the shop knew very well.

She said that it would be hard for the woman now. The boy had helped her on their little farm and now she had no one. Stan wished he hadn't asked. It wasn't his fault. It was Errol, who was supposed to tie him up. It was Errol who let him escape. It was Errol who had chased him. So why did he feel so guilty? They didn't even need to do anything with the kid in the first place. He wouldn't have done anything.

All Stan wanted to do was to get back to his own son and give him a squeeze. He'd never been overly affectionate with him, not wanting him to be soft, but he thought that might change now. The one thing that Stan was certain about, he didn't want his little boy following in his old man's footsteps.

He wondered if it was too late to change himself. Be something that the little fella could be proud of, he thought. Yeah, great. What else could he do? Everything he had ever done in his life had lead him back to doing jobs like this one. The thing that frightened him was if he did any more time inside. He knew that would be an end to his relationship with the boy. The kid's mother had said as much. And he found it hard to disagree with her logic.

He'd been thinking about it a lot. Getting out. He knew it wouldn't be easy. The boss wouldn't let him go if he asked. He'd be worried about grassing. Stan knew too much. But Stan knew he'd never grass the boss or any of the others, but it wouldn't be easy to convince the boss of that. He knew of one other bloke who wanted out. They never saw him again.

He could take off. That was the easy way out. But it meant he couldn't ever go back to London. They'd watch his boy. The boss knew about him. Stan didn't think they'd hurt him or his ex. They might ask her a few questions, threaten her, but if he didn't tell her anything, his ex wouldn't have anything to hide.

But then, where would he go. An ex-crim with no other skills. He knew he could be a welder or something like that. He'd always been good with his hands. Maybe he could do a trade. He wasn't that old. He could show them that he'd work hard. And then when he got himself sorted, he could let the ex know where he was. They'd have stopped looking for him by then. And he could see his boy. And his boy would know his old man wasn't a loser. He liked the sound of that.

The two men turned in for a few hours sleep.

When Stan's alarm went off at two o'clock he felt like he'd barely slept at all. His eyes felt gritty. He shook Errol awake.

"What the fuck." Errol's standard response.

"Come on, let's get this done."

They climbed into the van without another word. Nothing moved in the town. Errol was driving, something Stan never enjoyed. He drove too fast. But if Stan said anything, Errol would go faster.

The road was windy. They rounded a bend, something danced out of the shadows of the road-side. Errol yelled, "shit," and hit the brakes, but not fast enough to avoid whatever-it-was from connecting with the side of the van.

"What the fuck was that?"

They both climbed out. Stan walked back behind the van and could see something lying in the middle of the road. As he got closer he realised it was some sort of deer. Errol came up behind him. The deer was still alive. It lay on its side, kicking with its back legs, in a feeble attempt to rise. It's flank was rising and falling in tandem with its frantic breathing. There was a big wound on its side. A rivulet of blood ran into the road side.

"Come on, let's go," said Errol.

"We can't leave it like this."

"What are you gonna fuckin' do with it, you tosser. You got a gun, or are you gonna bandage it up and give it a cuddle. Don't be a weak idiot." Errol turned and headed back to the van.

Stan stood, staring down at the deer. He turned and followed Errol. Errol was standing near the front of the van. There was glass on the road and only one headlight was working. There was a blood smear on the van.

"Fuckin' prick of a thing."

"Errol, you're a bastard."

They climbed into the van and drove away.

The village was as quiet as the town. Errol had stopped at the top of the final rise, turning off the unbroken headlight, before they saw the village. They sat looking down into the few streets. Errol drove quietly down, turning onto the road to the ruins. They stopped in the car park.

"Hang on, don't get out," said Stan, who pulled the cover off the internal light and pulled out the bulb, dropping it into the ash tray.

"Right, door open, quietly."

"Fuck you," was Errol's input.

The piece they needed was easy to access, but larger than the other two. They grunted as they heaved it up out of the grass. Stan walked backwards, rocking from side to side with the short steps the heavy piece forced them to take.

"Fuck, why didn't you open the door before," grunted Errol.

They were forced to put the piece down and open the rear door. They hefted it again, sliding it onto the cloth-wrapping they had used on the other pieces. Stan pushed the door closed as quietly as he could. The sound was enough to make a dog start barking in the village. Shortly after a light came on in one of the houses.

The men jumped into the van.

"Don't drive like an idiot."

"Fuck off."

Errol drove carefully back up the road with his lights off, switching them on only when they topped the rise heading out of town.

The deer struggled and thrashed as the van approached. Errol didn't slow, he swerved around it at the last second, laughing as he did. They carried the final piece into the garage, lying it on the floor beside the other two. Stan took out the mobile phone.

Eve's phone was set to vibrate, she didn't want the kids to wake when the text came in. The short buzz against the bedside table was enough to wake her. She smiled in the darkness when she read the single word, 'done'.

Sergios didn't know what had woken him. He hadn't been sleeping well since the pieces were taken. He was surprised by how much it had affected him. It was guilt, but he knew this was a silly reaction to have. He could not have done anything to prevent the theft. But it left him feeling hollow. This was his heritage, and that of his children and grandchildren. He wished he could do more.

He could hear his neighbour's dog barking. It wasn't unusual, he barked sometimes. Sergios knew he wouldn't sleep. His wife's deep breathing continued without pause. Nothing wakes her, he thought.

He swung his legs over the side of the bed, his feet falling instinctively into his slippers. He went to the kitchen and poured a glass of water from the tap, looking up towards the ruins as he did so. With a sliver of moon he could see the site backlit against the clear spring sky. Nothing looked amiss. He went to the toilet and then back to bed. The dog had stopped barking.

He woke early, far earlier than usual, before dawn. Something was nagging at him. He lay there thinking about being woken a few hours earlier. He knew he wouldn't relax until he checked the site. I should have done it last night, he thought.

His wife slept on.

He dressed and stepped outside and did something he hadn't done in years. He walked to the site. It was still dark, but he saw that sunrise was close, the promise of another clear day signalled in the east. As soon as he stopped in the car park, his breath coming in short bursts, he knew it was gone. His heart sank. I heard them he thought, and I did nothing.

"You fool," he said out loud. He hadn't taken his mobile with him. He walked as fast as he could back to the house and made several calls. The first was to Anna.

A sleepy voice answered.

"Anna, it's Sergios, a piece has gone from the site. It went only a few hours ago, I heard them. I think."

Anna sat bolt upright, wide awake, reaching for her notebook on the bedside table, as Sergios gave her the details of what had happened. She called the Captain immediately afterwards.

"Go there and see if you can see anything."

Anna dressed quickly, climbing into the patrol car she had driven home the night before. The sun was still behind the hills, but daylight had broken, as Anna headed out of the main town towards the village. When she saw the deer she started to deviate around it but then stopped. It was still alive. She could see glass on the edge of the road.

She looked at the deer. It's movements were barely discernible, she knew it was close to death. She took out her service revolver and shot it through the head. It was the first time she had fired her weapon outside of the shooting range at the training college in Athens.

Deer were a problem on the island's roads. They were shy creatures. But with little road sense. They would come out of nowhere, darting in front of vehicles. A tourist had died the previous year, colliding with one while riding a scooter. Anna dragged the carcass off the road. Before she got back into the car she picked up several of the biggest pieces of broken glass, and then continued to the village. Sergios was waiting at the site when she arrived. The pair stood looking at the place where the missing piece had been.

"Do you know, it had probably been there for hundreds of years on the ground. It had been in that spot as long as I can first remember. And even then it looked like it had been there for a long time."

Anna understood that the old man was upset by the recent thefts.

"Yes, it is very sad." It was all she could think to say.

"Come, my wife has made coffee for us."

They walked the short distance to Sergios' house.

"I will come in shortly, let me call the Captain."

Anna explained that there was nothing to see at the site, but told the Captain about shooting the deer.

"It's possible that whomever stole the piece, also hit the deer," she said. "It's likely the passenger side headlight that is damaged. And there would likely be blood and damage to the body of the vehicle." She added.

"Yes, that's good," her boss responded. "I'll have the other men keep a look out. I'll see you at the station this morning."

26

Eve woke feeling relaxed and a little excited. Those idiots did it. Thank god for that she thought. And now to get out of here.

She reached for her phone and sent a text to the dolts telling them to meet her in the usual place. She was tempted to catch a bus to the town, to inspect the final piece. It was the best of the three. But she knew it wouldn't be smart to go to the house. She would have all the time in the world to admire them in London. And she would do that. It was a thing she did. She had a camping chair at the warehouse and she would make sure no-one else was around before making herself comfortable in front of the piece and simply admire it for a time. Soaking in every detail, before she packaged it up for shipping.

The movement of the pieces was where her London associate proved vital. Eve doubted she'd be able to do it without him. She'd briefly considered it early on when she realised how much his services were costing her. But she quickly realised that it was a complicated business. It was a business he had built over a life time. She knew that she was only one of many clients. It required a world of contacts and connections in places from customs services to airlines and shipping companies. And it required something else from time to time. Muscle.

This was a crude but necessary part of the operation, as Eve saw it. She knew her associate had no qualms about employing persuasion where it was necessary. It was something she was never required to know about. It was rarely referenced in their discussions, and when it was, only in vague terms.

Eve dressed and walked downstairs and asked Althaia if her assistant was able to watch her kids after breakfast for half an hour. She had used the young woman's services on several occasions during her stay, so she could meet with the two men, but using the excuse that she wanted go for a walk by herself.

"I want one last walk around the village before I go," she said to Althaia.

"Of course, Miss Eve, is no problem. She is upstairs cleaning room one. Please ask her."

Once the maid had agreed to watch the kids, Eve sent a text to the dolts and told them to meet her at the usual spot at nine.

"Mr Terry, Mr Terry. I have a call for you. Mr Terry."

I woke with a start.

"Okay Althaia, I'm coming.

I padded across to the door in my boxer shorts. Althaia held out her mobile when I opened the door, looking off to the side, her modesty prevailing.

"It is Anna, from the police."

"Thanks Althaia, I'll bring your phone down when I'm finished."

I saw the look of disappointment on Althaia's face as I shut the door. I knew she would be keen to listen to what we discussed. But I didn't think it was a good idea.

"Anna, it's Terry."

"Terry, I wanted to tell you that another piece was taken from the small village on the north coast. Have you seen this woman, Eve, today?"

"No. I haven't. But I'll let you know when I do. I'm helping her with her bags this evening. She's on the late ferry."

"Okay. That is good. Let me know if she says anything, is it the right word, pertinent?"

"Yes," I smiled. "Pertinent is the right word. I will definitely let you know."

"Also, something else." She explained about the dead deer and the likelihood of a damaged vehicle. "It is probably nothing but keep watch, if you will."

"I certainly will."

"Good bye," was all she said before breaking the connection.

I looked at the time. Eve would probably be having breakfast. I dressed quickly and headed down to Maria's, dropping Althaia's mobile back to her on the way.

"Everything is okay?"

"Yes, she had another question about my visit to the ruins. It was nothing very interesting."

Eve was sipping coffee when I walked in. Her kids were already on the sand below, playing in the shallows.

"Good morning, join me," she said.

"Hi."

Maria smiled when she came to the table.

"Your usual?"

"Thanks Maria."

I ploughed straight in.

"Another piece was taken last night."

Eve sat up in her chair. "That's terrible. Where from?"

"A village on the north coast."

"I bet I know the place you mean. I visited those ruins. It's a beautiful spot. How did you find out so soon?"

I didn't want to say that I had the local police-woman calling me.

"Althaia told me. Her brother is from up there."

"Yes, I remember her saying that." She nodded, her coffee cup held in two hands in front of her.

Eve finished her coffee, and looked at her watch.

"I'll see you a little later," she said.

She collected the kids and headed back to the hotel. I watched her go. Something nagged. I followed.

With the children sorted, Eve walked to the edge of the village along the road. She could see the van in the distance. As she drew closer she noticed the broken headlight straight away. Her relaxed mood started to dissipate.

"What happened to the headlight?"

Errol was driving. Stan had made sure, leaping into the passenger seat ahead of the other man.

"Hit a deer last night."

"That's all?"

"Yeah missus, that's all, it's not a problem. We've got the new piece, all safe and sound."

"Good. Good. Get to the harbour at seven, as we discussed. I don't want to see or hear from you again, unless it's absolutely necessary. Got it?"

"Sure missus. It's all good."

Eve turned and walked off without a further word.

"What a fuckin' bitch," said Errol.

I listened to her go into her room with the kids and shut the door before I climbed the stairs. I went into my room and waited quietly. I heard her speaking to Sofia, Althaia's off-sider, and then I heard footsteps in the corridor. I had not bolted the door and opened it quietly, just a crack, in time to see Eve walking towards the stairs.

I gave her time to leave the building before heading down, peeking around the corner to see Eve heading off up the street towards the edge of village. I wonder?

I walked quickly to the beach and then along the sand, going as fast as possible without running and drawing attention to myself. I found the spot where I had walked through the grass previously and headed towards the road, cutting back at the last minute to the place from which I had seen Eve talking to someone in the van. The van was there, and so was Eve. I could hear her voice but not anything she said. It was very frustrating, but I was scared to move any closer.

Shortly afterwards she headed back towards the village. The van started and then turned around. I waited until the last moment and then stepped out onto the road. There were two white men in the van. But it was hard to make out any details through the tinted windscreen. The thing that really caught my eye, the van had a broken passenger-side headlight.

The man in the passenger seat stared at me as they drove past. I looked away.

I was bursting with the need to speak to Anna but I didn't want Eve to see me on the road, so I went back to the beach the way I had come. I asked Althaia if I could borrow her phone again. She gave me a quizzical look, but handed it to me without a word.

"Anna, it's me."

"Yes, hello."

"Anna, I saw her talking to the men in the van again. I couldn't hear anything. But they were two white men. I mean, they didn't look Greek. And Anna, the van had a broken headlight.

Anna said nothing for a moment.

"Did you get the registration number?"

"Shit, sorry, no. I was too busy looking at the headlight."

"Okay, this is important, I must go, thank you."

My pulse was racing. It felt like that first night, when I had hiked to the ruins. But what could I do now? I walked back inside and put Althaia's mobile on the office counter. Thankfully she was speaking with a customer and could only look at me before I turned and departed.

"Captain," said Anna, walking into her boss' office, "I just had another call from the Australian. He says he has seen the woman, Eve, speaking with two men in a van outside the port village, as before. He said that the van had a broken headlight."

The Captain looked down at his big hands, bouncing his fingertips against each other.

"I will go and speak with her."

"Should I come with you?"

"No. Stay here in case I need anything from you."

The Captain stood and walked out, setting his cap in place.

Eve frowned when her phone rang, but then realised it wasn't the dolts.

"One of my officers reported that you were seen meeting with men in a van."

Eve was horrified, her heart rate had risen.

"Who saw me, who told you?"

"It was the Australian. He also reported that the van had a broken headlight. We know about the dead deer."

"How did he know about the dead deer?"

"My officer must have told him. I will look after that. All you have to do is leave. You go tonight?"

"Yes."

"And everything goes with you." It didn't sound like a question to Eve.

"Yes."

"Keep the van out of sight for the day, do not drive it anywhere before evening, you hear me? If you do, I may not have control over what happens."

"Understood."

The Captain broke the connection.

Eve put the phone on the table. So, she thought, Terry is following me. And he seems to have some sort of connection with the Greek policewoman.

She punched the pre-set for the dolts and then cut the connection. She had read too many stories about people being arrested on the strength of what they said over a mobile phone. She'd have to go and see them quickly. She looked at her watch. The bus. She sent a text, 'one of you, museum, thirty minutes.'

Eve got her kids out the door in record time. The bus drove past the door as she walked down the stairs. Luckily it was heading into the village and would stop near the jetty, where it would turn around for the journey to the capital.

Captain Danellis put his mobile down in the centre console of his car. He was not happy. He didn't like loose ends. This issue with the deer and the headlight—and the Australian for that matter—were loose ends. Who was this person, he wondered. Some amateur sleuth? Whatever, he was making this far more complicated than it should be.

But hopefully it would be at an end tonight and his bank balance would be a little fatter than it had been. Not that the extra money would appear in his bank account, that would be stupid. He didn't get to where he was by being stupid.

This was only the second time his relationship with the man in London had involved removing things from the island. No, bringing things to the island, that was much more his usual connection with the man. It was an intermittent arrangement. In this case it was the first time he had heard from the man in over a year. But that was how it was. He would need to keep an eye on his smart, young policewoman. She was perhaps a little too smart. He drove around for a while and then back to the office. He called Anna in and did not invite her to sit.

"I am not very happy with all this," his tone and gaze were stern. "I have spoken to the woman. There is nothing to connect her to any of these robberies. She explained that the men in the van were merely asking directions. She does not know them. Thankfully, the woman was understanding and keen to help with our investigation, otherwise she might have made trouble for us. Your judgement in this instance was not what it might have been. Let's not trouble her again with this."

Anna didn't know what to say. The Captain looked at her.

"Should we search the vehicles going on the ferry tonight?"

"Because the woman is leaving tonight? She is not leaving by vehicle, is she?"

"Well, no, but we know the thieves are still on the island, whether or not she is a part of it, they may try and remove the pieces tonight."

"No," the Captain said after a pause. "There is nothing to be gained by this, except upsetting the ferry lines and the tourists. Go. Enough."

Anna walked out. Crushed.

Even if the woman wasn't involved, which Anna was still in two minds about, it still made sense to search the vehicles going on to the ferry. There would only be a handful, she thought. And given the size of the pieces, it wouldn't take long to see if anyone was trying to move them.

27

I heard Eve go past my door with her kids and down the stairs. I stepped out onto my balcony to see which way they went, and watched them walk up and board the bus. Why stop now, I thought. I sprinted down stairs and turned the corner up the hill and across the plaka. I prayed he was home.

Stavros looked surprised to see me, especially red-faced and panting.

"Writer?"

"Stavros, I need your help. Is urgent. Can you drive me to the capital?"

"Of course." He didn't hesitate or ask me why.

"Can we hurry, please, and bring your mobile phone." He pulled the door shut. His ancient Citroen was parked at the side of his house. It didn't look like it was up to the journey. The canvas roof was torn, the body work faded, scratched and full of dents. And where the rear seat should have been was evidence of the big man's vocation: nets, boots, boxes and ropes.

He climbed in, the car listing heavily to port. My weight didn't go far to bringing balance to the whole affair. He cranked the starter and the old machine roared into life, a plume of dark smoke spewing from the exhaust.

When we exited the village, I could see the bus towards the top of the pass ahead of us.

"Can you catch the bus?"

Stavros pushed his foot down, the old car shook and rattled as it moved beyond its best safe speed. Thankfully the bus was not in much better shape and we began to make ground.

I wondered what I should tell Stavros. I looked across at him and he smiled and pushed his foot a little harder, but said nothing. It gave me a strange feeling in the pit of my stomach to know how much trust and faith this big man was placing in me.

We gained on the bus and I told Stavros to slow down a little, holding a healthy, but not huge gap. I asked him for his phone above the roar of wind through the roof and the bellow of the tired engine. He passed it to me without question. I dialled Anna's number.

"Anna, it's me,"

She asked me to wait.

"I have walked outside so no-one can hear me."

"Listen, Eve has headed to the main town on the bus. I'm not sure she's up to anything, but I thought I would follow her, just in case. I'm in a car, of sorts, with someone from the village."

"Terry, you should not do this. My Captain is very angry. He says he has spoken to this woman and there is no issue. He says you and I must stay away from her."

"Well, I'm not so convinced. But whatever, I'm not going to do anything, just keep an eye on her. Are you in the main town?"

"Yes, that is where the police station is."

"I will call you again." I broke the connection before she could say anything further.

Stavros was smiling and seemed to be enjoying the outing.

"Thank you," I said.

"Is nothing."

The bus stopped neared the plaka and I asked Stavros to pull up a distance away. What should I tell him?

"You wait for me?"

"Ok, I wait."

Still no questions.

I walked along the street, walking past a line of cafes and tourist shops opposite the plaka. I could see Eve and the kids. She crossed the plaka and I crossed the road, trying to keep as many people as possible between us.

She walked down a street running off the plaka, seemingly heading towards the museum we had visited days before. I waited on the corner of the street, ducking back as she turned to look behind. She seemed worried about being followed. What did she know or suspect?

I gave it a few seconds and dared another look. She was almost at the other end of the street. The museum was just around the corner. I walked down the street to the next corner, where a group of tourists stood beside a small bus. My heart was racing.

I peeked around the corner. Eve stood only twenty metres away, talking to someone. Even though it was only a short glimpse, I was convinced it was the man who had stared at me from the van. I walked into the shop on the corner from where I could watch the proceedings through the window without being seen.

Eve hated the idea of taking her kids near these idiots, they had not had anything to do with them and she'd wanted to keep it that way.

But, as she saw it, it was less of a risk than speaking over a mobile phone.

She was pleased to see that it was the least offensive of the pair who had come along. She couldn't remember which one he was, and didn't really care. She intended keeping the meeting as brief as possible, she was wary that anyone might see her.

She had kept an eye out to see if Terry was following. She had seen the old car in the distance behind the bus, but it was a bit rustic for a tourist, so never gave it a second thought. And she'd checked a couple of times while she was walking through the town, but couldn't see him anywhere.

She had a quick conversation with Stan and then turned and headed back to the plaka.

I turned away when Eve about-faced. She and the kids headed back towards the plaka. I decided to follow the man. I ducked out of the shop when Eve had gone past the door and turned around the corner towards the museum. The man was walking away from me down the street. I maintained the distance. He crossed the road and turned into another street. I crossed and then waited on the corner, daring a look. There were no tourists in this part of the town and he would see me if he turned. I waited briefly and then turned the corner. He was gone. Bugger.

I walked quickly down the street. Half-way along, a smaller street cut across. I turned left. It was a residential area. Blocks of units ran the entire length to where the street bent around to the left and abruptly ended, another building blocking my path. There was no sign of the man. I turned and walked quickly back and crossed over to follow the street in the other direction. This way the street bent around along the side of a hill, opening out with houses running along the top side.

I couldn't see him here either. I wasn't sure what to do.

Stavros. I'd better get back to him and started to turn when something caught my eye.

It was a white van, parked in the driveway of one of the houses. It was pointed away from me so I couldn't see if it had a broken headlight. I started to walk to towards it when the front door of the house opened.

"She wants us to put the van in the garage," said Stan, walking through the front door. "Something about keeping the broken headlight out of sight until dark."

"Bollocks to that."

"Should I call her and pass on your message, or will you do it yourself?" Stan was getting a bit sick of the attitude from Errol.

"Bollocks to you as well."

"Look, I don't reckon she's tellin' the full story. She reckoned she came to town to finalise details for tonight. But she'd already sorted that. How many times had she told us? Why would she come all this way to tell us? What's she worried about? I wonder if someone might be on to us? I asked her if she was worried about anything, and she said she had a contact in the cops, that there was nothing to worry about, but I'm not so sure."

For once Errol replied without an insult or curse. Stan had his attention.

"Alright, let's get it under cover."

The two men walked out of the house and opened the garage door. They'd need to move the pieces out of the way to get the van inside.

"We might as well load it now, while we're at it," said Stan.

"Good idea, back the van up to the doorway, so no-one can see us."

Stan turned the van around and then reversed it back up to the garage. The rear door opened far enough for them to slide the pieces into the back and cover them.

Errol shut the door and Stan finished reversing the van into the garage.

Stan pulled the door closed and both men returned to the house.

What went into the van? It was definitely something weighty and long. Too much of a coincidence?

I pulled out Stavros' phone and called Anna again.

"Anna, it's me. Eve got off the bus and met a guy near the museum. I followed the guy after she left. He went back to a house a few streets away. I saw a white van there and I watched while they loaded something heavy into it and then parked it in the garage."

I paused. Anna didn't respond straight away.

"Terry, I must think about this. Stay where you are." She broke the connection.

What do I do? wondered Anna. The Captain will not like me speaking to him again about his, after he told me to leave it. But this is something that is worth pursuing.

She knocked on the Captain's door. He looked up, not especially happy to see her standing there.

"Yes," he said in a clipped tone.

"Captain, I must tell you this." She explained about the calls from Terry and the men at the house with the van. She hoped that once he had heard the evidence he might soften towards her persistence. She was wrong.

He drew a long breath, his hands joined under his chin, his index fingers pointing up like a gun across his lips towards his nose. His voice was calm, but his eyes were locked on Anna's.

"So, you have been a police officer for what, three years?"

Anna didn't like where this was going.

"Yes, but..."

He cut her off.

"So, after so much experience you believe that you know better than I, about policing matters?"

"No, no. But I think that the evidence..."

He cut her off again, separating his hands and raising a finger to forestall her next comment.

"So with all this vast experience. Tell me what evidence we have that a crime has been committed?" He continued before she could speak. "I'll tell you what evidence we have. We have no evidence. I have spoken to the woman at length and there is nothing in what she has told me that would suggest she is involved in a crime on this island. And you have the testimony of a foreign national, making wild accusations about this woman. My understanding is that he is smitten with her. She has most likely rebuffed his advances and is trying to make trouble for her. Whatever the case, there is nothing to suggest her involvement."

"I have admired your work to this point. Do not make me question this. I want you to go and see this Australian and tell him that if he calls you again, I will come and visit him. And this he will not enjoy. I will have him on the next ferry from the island or on a charge for wasting the time of the Greek police. Do you understand? Are you comfortable with implementing this order?"

She nodded.

"I'm sorry, I didn't hear you." He leant forward turning his head to the side.

"Yes sir."

"And after you have spoken to this person, I want you to come back and write a full report of your actions in this case and have this on my desk by tomorrow morning. Am I being clear?"

"Yes sir."

"Good. That is good. You are dismissed."

Anna felt like she'd been felled with a hammer. What have I done? she thought. She knew she had been lucky to work with an officer of the Captain's experience, but it was more than this. He treated her as he treated the male officers. It was a great opportunity for her and now she had ruined it. She wanted to cry, but would not do that.

She walked out to the footpath and called Terry.

"Hello."

"Terry, it is Anna. Meet me in the plaka in five minutes." She broke the connection before he had a chance to say anything. It was only a short walk for Anna.

I saw her as soon as I entered the plaka, she was standing in the centre, arms folded. She watched me approach.

"Anna, you have to come and…"

She raised her hand.

"Stop," she said. She sounded angry. "You must stop."

I stood open-mouthed, but said nothing.

"Please do not tell me anything further. I am in trouble with the Captain. In fact we are both in trouble. He says if you do not stop contacting me then he will have you removed from the island or arrested."

She paused and continued.

"I am sorry, but that is how it is. You must stop following these people and you must stop calling me."

I was dumbfounded.

"Anna, there is something here. I am convinced they've stolen the pieces from the sites. And I'm convinced they're involved in the death of Alfio. How can you ignore that? How can your Captain ignore that?"

"Terry, you have no evidence. I have only your word on these things. I appreciate your interest and your effort, but you have nothing. And it must stop now. You must go back to your village and enjoy your holiday, write your books, and stop being a detective. It is for both of us that you should do this."

She looked no happier than me. It was clear she wasn't enjoying this.

"Anna, I will stop, I promise. I just want you to look me in the eye and tell me that you—not your Captain—that you believe that I am not onto something. That these people are not involved in something illegal."

She sighed, her lips pushed together, the air escaping from her nose.

"It does not matter what I believe. I have my orders and I must obey them."

I was losing her, I could feel it.

"Anna, Eve leaves tonight. You know the van will go with them tonight on the ferry, don't you? And the artefacts will be gone as well. The artefacts that belong to the people of this island and to all Greek people, they will be gone, to some rich person."

It was as passionate a speech as I could muster, but it wasn't finished.

"And worse than that. The people responsible for the death of an innocent boy. A boy who did nothing but help his mother and herd his goats. His killers will have escaped punishment. Can you live with that?"

She said nothing for many seconds. Her eyes clouded but no tears escaped.

"I must go." She spun on her heel and walked off without another word. I stood watching her go.

Stavros. I had kept him waiting for too long. He waved when he saw me approaching.

"All is okay?" he asked.

"No Stavros, it's not all okay." I didn't know what to do or say to the big man. "Let's go home."

He started the car and turned back the way we had come, a plume of dirty smoke in our wake.

Eve sat at a cafe on the side of the Plaka, her kids enjoying their ice creams. She had watched him speak with the policewoman and then walk to the old car and climb in.

"Bastard," she muttered through pursed lips. She'd seen that he came from the direction of the museum and wondered if he had seen her with the dolt. The only thing that gave her comfort was the body language that the policewoman had displayed towards him when they spoke, abruptly turning to leave, him looking forlorn as she left. She pulled out her mobile and called the Captain.

"I just saw your officer talking to the Australian. Are we on the same side here? He must have followed me again. You led me to believe that there would be no further problems." She was rarely this blunt with someone from whom she needed something.

"Please do not speak to me this way. Let me be very clear with you. These fools you employ seem to go out of their way to get caught. This is the second time I have had to deal with this issue because of them. It is you that should answer the question as to which side you are on. I have done my job. In fact I have done more than my job. Might I suggest this be reflected in my fee."

"I have fixed the issue of the young policewoman and the Australian. She was doing what I ordered her to do. Breaking ties with him and telling him to mind his business. Please do not tell me how to do my job. I would ask that you focus on yours and leave the island without any further troubles."

Eve knew when she was beaten.

"I am sorry if it sounded like I was questioning your actions. I was certainly not doing that. And I am thankful for your help. I will ensure that there is a little extra on top of your fee. I will not trouble you again."

The Captain put his phone on the desk, leant back in his chair, linking his fingers behind his head, a smile on his face.

Eve didn't smile. The call had cost her money. But at least, she thought, things are under control.

28

It was clear to me that Anna was as troubled about what was going on as me. I'm no cop, but I would have thought there was enough suspicion to at least check what was in the house or the van. Why was her boss being such a bastard?

And then it hit me. What if he was in on it? I threw my head back in an 'of-course' moment.

Stavros looked across at me. We were still driving back to the village, at a more sedate pace than the trip to town, the wind whistling a little less vigorously through the rents in the roof.

"Stavros, I think I know who stole the things from the ruins."

The big fisherman scowled.

"You know who is stealing from my island?"

"And I think they might also have been involved with Alfio's death."

The big man slammed a palm into the steering wheel. I was surprised it didn't break. If I was concerned about Stavros struggling to understand what I had said, I needn't have worried.

"Who? We must do something."

"I don't know what to do. I have told the police. I was talking to them in the town."

"How is you know this thing?"

"Stop the car."

Stavros pulled over to the side of the road. We were parked on top of the final hill before the village. It was laid out below us in all its glory. The harbour, the boats, the white houses and hotels. It really was beautiful.

I started to explain to Stavros what I knew. I told him everything, including my interactions with Eve, the bracelet, the bear, everything. It took a while. I had to explain much of it a few times over so he could understand. Eventually he had the whole story.

We sat quietly for a time, staring down towards the village. The midday ferry was pulling into the harbour. It cleared the break-water, swinging into a tight arc to stop alongside the jetty. The manoeuvre left a huge letter 'U' of churned water.

"She leave tonight?"

"Yes, she leaves tonight."

"But not in car."

"No, I will help her to carry her baggage and the children. There is no car for her."

He looked at me like he didn't understand what I had said.

"Why do you help?"

"Look…it's complicated. I liked her to begin with. But then when I thought something was happening, I wanted to stay close and watch her." I wondered if he would understand this.

He smiled. "Like what Sun Tzu say?"

I pulled back, a little flummoxed.

"The Japanese general?"

"No, Chinese. He talk about enemy. Keep them close to you, like friend."

"Yes, yes, it was just like that." The big man kept on surprising me.

"So, we cannot talk to police?"

"No, we cannot."

"What about Sergios? Brother to Althaia."

Of course. I had forgotten about Althaia's brother and his work on the island.

"Yes, lets talk to him. That's a great idea."

Shame on me for underestimating this brooding brute of a man.

We parked at Stavros' house and walked back to the *Cycladaen*. Althaia looked up and smiled when we walked in.

"Hello you two," she said in English.

I had suggested to Stavros that maybe we should not say anything to Althaia about my suspicions. I had messed up enough times on my dealings with Eve, that I still had doubt nagging at me from time to time. He thought this was sensible.

"Hi Althaia, I wanted to ask your brother about some of the ruins. Would it be okay to get his number from you?"

"Yes, yes, of course. He speak very good English, better than me."

She wrote the number on a piece of paper and we walked to Maria's place to have a coffee and speak to Sergios. Thankfully both Maria and Petros were busy with customers.

"Sergios," was how he answered his mobile.

"Sergios. My name is Terry. I am staying at Althaia's Hotel. I met you the other day when you were here to ask about the stolen objects."

"Yes, yes. I remember you. You are the writer. Althaia talks about you."

"Yes, that's me. Look, I'm here with Stavros, and I wanted to talk to you about the stolen pieces."

"Terry, I am actually driving my car, and not far from your village. Why don't I come to speak with you, how do you say, in person."

"That would be great, we are sitting at Maria's taverna, the same place where I met you before."

Sergios arrived within fifteen minutes.

"Sergios," I said, rising from my chair and offering my hand.

"Terry," he said to me, and then spoke to Stavros in Greek.

"This sounds intriguing Terry, what did you wish to say?"

"Why don't we order you a coffee, this may take a while," I said.

Maria came over when she saw Sergios, to say hello. And then went off to get him a coffee.

"Right," I said, and went through the whole story again, from start to finish. Sergios' English proficiency made it a much faster task than with Stavros.

"This is incredible," were his first words.

"I have only spoken to the police, Stavros and you about this. Unfortunately the police do not seem interested."

"And you think these people are involved in the death of poor little Alfio."

"I do."

"This woman, this Eve, she will leave on the ferry tonight? And you think that these men in the van will leave on the same ferry tonight?"

"Yes, yes I do."

"I shall talk to the police."

I raised my hand. "No, I'm not sure that is a good idea. The Captain has already threatened to arrest me if I contact them again. Anna, the policewoman you were here with, is already in trouble because of me. I don't think contacting the Captain or Anna will do us any good."

I didn't add that I had my suspicions about the Captain's involvement in the crimes.

"I am happy you have told me this, but if we cannot involve the police, what can we do?"

"I honestly don't know."

I jumped at a sudden noise. Stavros had slapped the table top with his catcher's mitt-sized palm.

"We must look." Sergios and I turned towards the big man. Stavros' face was clouded in anger.

"We must stop the men and the car," he added.

"The ferry goes to Athens from here," I said, "do you have police contacts in Athens? Someone could intercept them when they arrive."

"If we explain this to someone in Athens, they will want to contact the Captain, it will not be good for you. Or me."

"We need to have a look inside that van. We can't go to the house. So that leaves the ferry," I said. "What if I buy a ticket and travel on it. I could go down and check their car after the ferry departs, while they're sitting upstairs. If the pieces are there, I can contact you and you could tell someone that they're definitely in the car. Someone would have to do something then."

Sergios and Stavros both looked concerned.

"This could be dangerous for you," said Sergios.

"Yes, dangerous," echoed Stavros, whose eyes were narrow slits as he focused on understanding the English being spoken.

"Is there a better plan? What else can we do?"

Neither man responded.

"I'd rather not do it," I said, "but we have to do something, and I can't think of anything better. The only thing is, that I'll need to borrow someone's mobile."

Stavros pushed his across the table without a word.

"Alright. I'd better go and buy a ticket. Wait here and I'll be back in a few minutes. We'd better talk about some options depending on how things work out."

I rose and walked to the street, just as Eve and her kids were heading back from the bus stop. Oh god, I thought, I was going to have to come up with some sort of excuse to leave on the ferry.

"Terry," said Eve, as I walked up to her.

"Hi Eve, almost time to go. What time should I come to your room to help with your bags?"

She gave me a strange look, like she was checking my face for sincerity or something else.

"Come at six," she said. "That should give us plenty of time."

"Okay, I'll see you then." I checked my watch. It was only an hour away. The sun had already disappeared behind the hills. The last light of day washed over the harbour.

The ferry office was near the end of the jetty. I bought a return ticket and walked back to the taverna where Stavros and Sergios sat staring at nothing, not speaking.

"What if van does not come?" asked Stavros.

I hadn't thought about that. I looked at the big man. He didn't often speak, but when he did what he said was usually worth hearing.

"I guess I won't get on the ferry. The problem is, she'll know I'm up to something."

"It would be better if she did not suspect. She can call the men and warn them. It would be better if I was on the ferry," said Sergios.

"No Sergios," Stavros and I said it simultaneously.

"It makes sense," said Sergios. "As you said, if you tell her you are leaving on the ferry and then do not, she will be very suspicious. She can call them. It will not be good. We will lose the pieces forever. I want to do this."

I didn't like it, but it did make sense. I looked at Stavros. He tilted his head to the side in a gesture suggesting acquiescence. I handed my ticket to Sergios.

"I must call my wife and tell her something. This will not be easy."

Sergios walked off to make the call. I watched him, his waving hands telling me he was going the hard sell on his wife but that she was not having a bar of it. He came back a few minutes later. He didn't look happy.

"That was not so good. But we must do this."

I checked my watch.

"I need to go and help Eve. I will see you at the ferry. Don't board until the very last. If we don't see the van then you won't need to go."

I walked back to my room, washed my face, and then went and knocked on Eve's door.

"Come in, it's open," she yelled. I walked in. She smiled. "You're a sweetie for doing this."

The bags were organised in the middle of the room.

"Okay you two," she said to the kids, "let's go."

I grabbed a big suitcase and headed down the corridor to the stairs, hefting the heavy bag down to the street below.

"Let's get going," said Stan. "It won't hurt if we're a bit early."

For once Errol didn't argue. They were both keen to get moving.

The van was already packed with their possessions. Stan was amazed at how lightly Errol travelled. The odour from his clothes suggested to Stan that perhaps Errol should rethink his strategy.

Stan checked the pieces one more time. As per the woman's instructions, they had wrapped them all in carpet underlay and then covered that with blue plastic tarpaulin tied with rope. Stan was happy with the job they had done and pushed the door closed. Errol was already in the driver's seat.

"You sure you should drive?"

"Fuck off."

"Look what happened last time. You want to have an issue now?"

"Fuck off."

It was dark as they drove through the town, heading for the road that crossed the island. Stan checked his watch again. He knew the woman would be heading towards the ferry. Like Errol, he would be relieved to see the back of her. She was not a nice person. They didn't even know her name. Stan had been in this business for most of his life and understood that people were hard, but the ones he went the extra yard for were the ones who had a bit of compassion, a hint of a smile, a shared joke. That didn't include this woman.

He sank back into the seat. Increasingly over recent days, when his mind was idle, his thoughts returned to Alfio. And not only Alfio. It was Alfio's mother, the people left behind, that Stan thought about as well.

His actions had shaped the future for a range of people, thought Stan. Death and killing had never bothered him, when it was some geezer on the receiving end. It was usually someone else in the business. Stan never sweated over that. He'd never actually had to do it himself, and doubted he could. But being around it, seeing it even, never really bothered him. But this was different. This bothered him.

Errol broke Stan's reverie, slapping him hard on the thigh.

"Come on matey, wake up, we're out of this fuckin' shit hole. We can get this pile of fuckin' rock on the boat and then start to relax. And in a day or so we'll be home. I can taste the Porter now." Errol licked his lips. It was the most animated that Stan had seen him since they arrived.

Stan didn't say anything.

"Alright, misery guts. What is it? You still thinkin' about spaz boy?"

"Don't call him that Errol. And yes, I was thinking about him. We really fucked up there."

"Look, it's what you call collateral damage. Unfortunate, but it happens. But let's not let it ruin our happy return home and the pile of lost-and-founds waiting for us." Errol took his hands off the wheel and rubbed them together.

Stan checked his watch.

"Don't drive too fast, we don't want to be sitting around too long and draw attention to ourselves."

Errol pushed the accelerator further to the floor in response but then eased up and smiled at Stan, his missing eye tooth giving Errol a maniacal leer.

"I'm glad you were here, I'm not sure I could have done that," said Eve, as she watched me struggle with the big suitcase. "It's a bit heavier than when I arrived. Must be all those artefacts I stole." She looked me in the eye as she said it. It was a second or two before she smiled.

She stopped to hug Althaia and say goodbye. Althaia smiled at me.

The ferry was coming past the break-water as we arrived at the end of the jetty. There were only a handful of foot passengers waiting behind the barrier, including Sergios. I didn't acknowledge his presence. Several vehicles, a couple of trucks and cars, waited to be loaded. There was no sign of the van.

Stan knew the port village was over the next rise and that the ruins were not far off to his right. It gave him a funny feeling in the pit of his stomach.

I squinted to see the drivers inside the vehicles. Window tinting and the darkness made it difficult. What I could see was only one person in each vehicle. None of them looked like the men I had seen.

The ferry went through its quick u-turn. The crew had the boarding ramp in place and waved the foot passengers forward in short order. The huge vehicle doors were also open and the first truck rolled forward.

"Thanks again," said Eve. "This is very kind. It was lovely to meet you. And as I said, if you're ever in London…"

I was a little distracted, glancing at the vehicles. It took me a moment to notice she was holding out her hand to me. I grabbed it clumsily.

"Yes, it's been nice. See you around."

"I look forward to your next book, I'll keep an eye out for it," she said as she herded the children up the ramp and onto the ferry.

Sergio waited near the bottom of the ramp. He looked at me and then towards the ferry. The crewman was waving him forward. The vehicle doors were still open, but there was no sign of the van. As they started to close I shook my head to Sergios and waved him back. The boarding ramp was pulled in, the ferry moved quickly along the break-water and out of the harbour.

Sergios fell in beside me. We watched the ferry disappear around the headland before we turned and walked back towards the street where Stavros waited.

Shit. What now?

"Slow up a bit, the turn is not far ahead. It's a tricky corner remember," said Stan.

"Anything for you, my old chum."

They clunked off the jagged edge of the paved road onto a dusty and rocky track. Errol slowed to a crawl, as they bumped their way down the steady gradient.

The three of us headed back to Maria's for a drink. We were all feeling deflated, no-one saying a word. Stavros' mobile, still in my back pocket, started to vibrate and then belt out *Zorba the Greek*. It made me smile. I looked at the screen, recognising the number.

"Anna?"

"Terry?"

"Yes, it's me."

Anna had taken a big risk.

She knew that if Captain Danellis found out what she was up to he would have her transferred, or worse, discharged from the Hellenic Police. It scared her a lot. Long before she set foot inside the academy in Athens she knew she wanted to be a police officer. Her training only reinforced it. It was obvious to her and to those around her that she was an intelligent woman and that promotion and opportunity within the service awaited.

So why am I risking that, she wondered? But she knew the answer. It was a big part of the reason she wore the uniform. She thought it would sound a bit corny to others, so it was something she never discussed, but even as a kid she had found herself supporting those who were unable to fend for themselves. The kids singled out for teasing, the ones a bit different to anyone else, the fat, the skinny, the tall, the short, the smart, the dumb. And while it would sometimes result in her being marginalised, in the end she had found herself, to her surprise, being looked up to by the majority.

More than a few of her teachers had commented to her parents or in her report cards that she was a natural leader, someone who inspired others. And while these traits might have taken her along any number of lucrative career paths it was the police service that drew her. She never had cause to question the decision for a moment.

That is what scared her about what she was doing. Putting that at risk before she had barely started. But, it was the inclination to follow her instincts, to right a wrong, that overpowered her concern for her career. It would always be this way for her.

And so she had found herself parked near the edge of the town, off duty and in her own car. She knew if the men were to take the van to the ferry, they would need to pass this point. She didn't know what she was going to do if they did pass by. She figured she could at least get the registration number and pursue that. She would follow them to the ferry and see if there might be an opportunity to look inside the vehicle. Not a great plan she thought.

She had only been waiting for half an hour when the van had driven by. She waited a long time before pulling out to follow. There would not be much traffic on the road at this time and she didn't want to spook them.

She had barely made the top of the first pass through the hills when her car, an old Renault—a graduation gift from her grandfather—had started to stutter in protest.

"No, not now," she yelled at it.

She had made the rise and could see the tail-lights of the van in the distance. Going down into the next valley was no issue. But as soon as she started to climb the next range, the protests started again.

"I promise, I will get a mechanic to fix you," she pleaded, "just not now." She made it to the final range before the Renault coughed and stalled, and would not restart.

She cursed and thumped the steering wheel. And she had no mobile signal. There was nothing for it, she decided. She climbed out and started to jog up the long climb to the top of the hill, the final one where she would be able to see the port village.

"I was following the van but my car stopped working. Have you seen the van? Did you see it go on to the ferry."

"No, we went to the ferry to see if the van came. We had a plan to get onto the ferry, but the van did not turn up here. Why didn't you let me know you were doing something, we could have planned this better?"

"I don't know. I had to do something but I didn't think I should involve anyone else. I am not in my police uniform. And I am driving my own car."

"Where are you?"

"I am on top of the hill looking down to the village."

"Stay there. We'll come and get you."

Sergios seemed to have understood most of what was said, but Stavros looked perplexed.

"We need to get Anna. Sergios, can we take your car? I can explain what happened on the way."

"Of course."

Sergios was parked at the end of the jetty. I was thankful he was here. His car was new and free of rubbish, and had a rear seat.

"Drive out of town, she is at the top of the first hill."

I explained what Anna had said, as we headed out of town. Anna was standing on the side of the road, watching us come towards her. She was all business and spoke in English for my benefit.

157

"I was following at a distance and then my car started not working well. I did not see them after the first hills. If you did not see them, they have taken another road between there and here."

"So where would they be going?" I asked.

"Well, they would not be putting the pieces back," said Sergios, referring to the road to the site above the port village. "That only leaves one other road. It heads to a small farming village in one of the earlier valleys."

"Maybe they are hiding the pieces," I said, "and then getting them later to remove them."

"Yes, that would make sense," said Anna. "Especially if they know we are suspicious."

"Should we drive back and look?" asked Sergios.

"What about track to cove?" It was Stavros.

"What do you mean?" I asked.

He broke into to Greek, looking out the open window at Anna.

"He says there is a rough track which turns off, back up the road behind me. That is goes to a small bay," said Anna.

I looked at Stavros, who shrugged.

Stavros spoke again to Anna.

"He says a boat could come to the cove and pick up the pieces, and take them to a larger boat."

"Shit," I said. "Should we go there first? If we're wrong, we'll know the pieces are still on the island."

"I agree," said Anna.

Anna climbed into the back with Stavros and we drove a few hundred metres up the road until Stavros said, "It is here."

Sergios eased the car onto the rough track and we began the decent towards the coast.

29

"Fuck," said Errol for the umpteenth time as they bounced over another huge rock.

"Try slowing down a bit, you don't want to bust something."

"Fuck off, or I'll bust YOU."

Stan shook his head.

The track began to flatten out as they neared the coastline. Rain had washed deep holes into sections. Stan thought they wouldn't be going any further if Errol drove into one. The track had narrowed, bushes rubbed along the van's sides, the scratching noises putting Stan's teeth on edge.

He breathed a huge sigh of relief when they stopped in a clearing of green grass, looking over a small beach and cove. Two huge headlands seemed to almost meet, giving the cove a lake-like quality. Once the engine was off, the only sound was the rustling of water gently disturbing the coarse sand.

"Wow."

"Fuck wow," sneered Errol, "where's the fuckin' boat. And we've gotta lift this shit down that bank." Errol's previous good humour had ebbed on the drive down. The fact that there was work to be done, only contributed to his funk.

"We're a bit early," said Stan. "Let's get the pieces down onto the beach so we don't waste time when they get here."

"If they get here. We don't know these fuckers. We don't even have a contact. That fuckin' bitch wouldn't tell us shit."

"Let's get it done."

Errol grumbled to himself as Stan opened the rear door. They hefted the first piece, carrying it to the edge of the clearing above the beach.

"Put it down for a sec, let's look for the easiest way down."

"Let's throw the fuckin' thing."

"Yes, do that. And then you can explain to the boss why it's in three pieces. Don't be an idiot." Stan was losing patience with his off-sider.

"Mr Tough Guy," was Errol's response.

Stan walked along the edge. It didn't look any easier anywhere.

"One of us'll have to ease them over the edge and the other one will have to go below to slide them down."

"I'm up top."

"Of course you are."

"Down you go."

"What, and climb up again to help you get each piece out of the van."

"Yeah, right, smart fucker, I meant after we get them out of the van."

"Of course you did, Errol. You're the thinker in this group."

"Want to say that again." Errol had stepped close to Stan.

"Grow up you idiot."

Errol's breath was coming in short bursts. He stared into Stan's eyes. The smell of Errol's breath made Stan want to gag.

"Again," was all Errol said.

The way Stan felt, he was tempted to give the fool a big shove in the chest but he knew where it would end up. Stan wasn't frightened of Errol, and would back himself in a stoush, but he knew now wasn't the time.

"Alright Errol, you win." Stan took a step back.

"Faggot."

They moved the remaining pieces to the edge, near the first one. Stan climbed down, grabbing roots sticking out of the sand, to slow his decent. It was further down than he'd estimated.

"You'll have to tie a bit of rope onto each one and hang onto to them until I can reach them. It's too far to let them go."

"Can't you catch them, you pussy."

"Errol, just do it, will you."

Stan watched as the end of the first piece appeared above him. It poked out and then dropped against the bank. The piece stopped briefly and then fell, careening straight at Stan. He dived to the side, the piece spearing into the sand right where he had been standing. It was upright. It stood for a moment and then tipped slowly, falling towards Stan. He had to roll out of the way a second time.

He sat up, spitting sand.

"Fuckin' rope. Burned my hand." Stan heard from above.

"You nearly killed me you fucking fool." Stan was furious.

"Calm down. It was an accident."

"You nearly killed me and you've probably broken it."

"Fuck off, it's sand. It'll be fine. Just pull it out of the way and I'll lower the next one."

This isn't going to end here, thought Stan. There'll be a reckoning.

Stan stood and dragged the piece towards the water and out of the way. It took all his strength to pull it through the cloying sand.

"Be fucking careful this time. If it happens again, so help me…"

"Yeah what? Gonna climb up and kiss me?"

Stan didn't say anything further, stepping back out of the way as he saw the next piece appear above him.

Errol managed the next piece more effectively. Letting it down slowly to where Stan was able to take some weight on the lower end. Once Errol felt Stan take the weight he let it go. The piece fell sideways and rolled the short distance to the bottom.

Stan was furious. He was about to yell when he heard a throaty growl behind him. He jumped around, a bright light blinded him. He threw up his hands in front of this eyes.

"Got something for us boys?" The voice was Irish.

"Can you point your light somewhere else," said Stan.

"Just checkin' to see who youse are. Never know who you might run across out here. But given you're lumpin' some big feckin packages down that cliff, I reckon I'm in the right place."

The light went out. When Stan's night vision started to return he could see the boat. Two men jumped out. One stood knee-deep keeping the boat off the sand.

The Irishman walked up to Stan.

"Let's get this shite on board."

I started to wonder if Sergios' car was going to make it. The sound of the underside scraping across the huge rocks was like fingernails on a blackboard. Having someone the size of Stavros in the back probably didn't help matters. It was taking a long time.

"How much further?" I asked after the racket of another scraping rock.

"More yet," came Stavros' succinct response. We hadn't discussed what we'd do if we found the men loading things into a boat. I was of the firm belief that the type of people who engaged in this kind of activity would probably be armed. Apart from having Stavros with us, we had nothing else to defend ourselves. Anna must have been thinking the same thing.

"When we get close, we must stop and go forward quietly. If they are here, they may be armed. Only thing we can do is call for support and get a description of the boat." She then spoke in Greek, explaining things to Stavros.

"Stavros says it is another kilometre or so. We should leave the car here, so anyone does not hear us. Sergios, maybe you wait with the car."

Sergios understood what Anna meant and was happy to stay behind. The three of us climbed out and started to move along the track on foot. I still had Stavros' phone and switched on the flashlight function.

Stavros said something in Greek. Anna laughed.

"He wonders how you did that."

We moved as quietly as we could. The track bent around through some short trees and then opened out into a clearing ahead. The van stood in the distance.

"Down," said Anna in a whisper. Once stopped, I could hear faint voices.

Anna spoke to Stavros in Greek.

"I tell him to wait here. He is big and easy to see. I tell him to come if we yell for him."

Anna and I continued forward in a crouch. There didn't appear to be anyone near the van. Once we got to the van we could see that the beach was down below the clearing. The voices were clear. We crawled forward to the edge.

"Don't you scratch me feckin boat or there'll be hell to pay." The voice was Irish.

The boat was a fast cruiser. I'd been whizzed around on a few of them when I was still selling books. A rich man's toy, or a smuggler's tool, maybe.

I could see four men, one in the boat, one holding the front of it off the beach, and two men in the water lifting something up to the one in the boat.

"Fuckin' heavy pile of rock," came another voice. They manoeuvred the heavy package into the boat.

The Irishman spoke again.

"Right, that's it then. Now, dere's been a change of plan. The trawler can't come in to get this stuff tonight. There's a Greek patrol boat gettin' about and the trawler captain is not keen to get into a spat with a boat with a big gun. We've got an island to stash the stuff on. The good news is you two fellas get to stay there with the stuff until the big boat comes. A holiday of sorts."

"You're fuckin' kiddin'. There's no fuckin' way we're staying on another fuckin' island."

"Well," said the Irishman—I thought he was very calm—"you'd best be takin' that up with ya boss. It was him that told me what was goin' on. I was brought in at the last, you might say. Things had to change."

"But as agreed, me offsider here, will take your van back on the ferry tomorra, and drop it off in Athens. All good there. Just you two fellas get some more island time. This one might be a little rough, but should only be for one night."

"Listen, ya mick fuck, we're not..." His words were cut short. I could see one of the men in the water go down. The other stood over him holding something near his throat.

"Now, I'm a patient man. But too a point. And when someone starts casting aspersions on me religion, well, that's a fraction beyond that point. Are you hearing me?"

The man lying in the water had taken on a different tone.

"Yes, yes, I hear you. Just don't cut me. I'm sorry. It's all fine."

"Ah, dat's what I like to hear. Common sense prevailing. And what about your mate up top there? Any problems?"

"No, no problems here."

"Good, let's be gettin' on with things then."

The two men climbed up the ladder, leaving only the last man at front.

"I'll be seein' ya in a day or two," came the lilt from somewhere in the boat, to the man in front. The big engines burbled into life and then the boat moved slowly backwards into deeper water, turned and then accelerated out between the headlands in a surge of white water. The man left behind turned to leave the water.

"Come on, let's go," whispered Anna. We both stood and moved quickly back in the direction of the car. Stavros stepped out of the shadows. I'd forgotten about him being there. I farted in surprise, my heart skipping a beat. Stavros let out a chuckle.

We were out of sight of the van.

"What'll we do if he comes driving along behind us?" I asked.

"Well, we can hide but that doesn't make it good for Sergios," said Anna. "Pray that he spends the night at the beach." We moved as quickly as we could. When we rounded the final bend and saw the car, there was still no sign of the van.

Anna spoke in rapid Greek. Sergios started the car before we were all in.

"So what do we do?" I asked Maria, after she had told Sergios and Stavros what had transpired, in Greek.

"I don't know."

"Shouldn't we call someone and tell them. The coast guard or something."

"But what do we tell them? We still do not know what was in that package, and we only saw one package," Anna's voice was flat. She sounded defeated. "I would have to speak to the Captain and he will be very angry with me. We need more proof than this."

"I know where they go." It was Stavros.

He continued on in Greek. He paused. Anna said to me in English. "He says that you also know where they will go."

I paused for a moment and then it clicked.

"Fuck, the little island. Oh, sorry Anna."

She ignored my apology.

"Why do you know?"

"I've been there with Stavros on his boat."

Stavros started speaking again in Greek.

"He says, that if they have a big trawler, it is the only small island where they could be close to the land."

"Yes, it has an old jetty." The car crunched over a big rock.

The climb up was as laborious as the decent and seemed to take an age. I think we all breathed a big sigh when we reached the tarmac road without incident.

"Down to the village," I said. "I think we've earned a drink. What about we go to Maria's and come up with a plan."

Listen to you, I thought to myself. Who was I, some fucking commando. This was getting crazy. I was a broken down author thinking he had super powers. No one said anything to the contrary, as Sergios pointed his little car down the hill towards the lights surrounding the peaceful harbour.

It felt like we'd been out all night. But it was still early, barely nine o'clock, as we took a table at Maria's place. There were several tables of other guests, it was the busiest I had seen it since my arrival. Maria darted over with a smile. Thankfully she didn't have time to stay and chat.

30

The big boat moved swiftly across the flat sea. The wiry Irishman's face was lit by the glare of the boat's electronics panel. It gave him a maniacal leer. Stan and Errol sat on the bench seat that ran along the back of the boat, the sound of the engines covering their conversation.

"This is fucking madness," said Errol.

"Madness it might be, but it's all we've got for now," said Stan. "You had your chance to suggest an alternative, but as I recall, it didn't go in your favour." Stan was feeling little better-disposed towards his partner than he was towards the Irishman.

"Yeah, fuck you very much."

"We're in this mess until someone picks us up."

"What are you boys whispering about back there?" The Irishman had turned to look at them. "I hope you're not entertaining any mutinous thoughts." The sound of metal on metal made the men look down to see that he was gently tapping an automatic pistol against the steering wheel.

"Now, one of you be good and go below and grab that bottle of

Jamesons and some glasses and we can all have a wee restorative, and den we'll all feel a bit better."

Stan walked forward, stepping around the three tarpaulin-wrapped packages on the deck. The sea was so smooth that Stan had no trouble moving about. The Irishman nodded with his head towards the louvered door beside him. Stan stepped down into the stateroom below. Despite his mind being occupied with thoughts of what might lay ahead, he couldn't help but be impressed by the spotless opulence of the boat. It was all wood panelling and white leather couches. There was a small kitchen on one side and another door. He checked several cupboards before finding the grog stash and the bottle of Irish whiskey. He took three shot glasses from another shelf and headed back to the Irishman.

"Dere now, dat's better. Dat's the business. A wee dram will do us a power of good."

Stan set the glasses down, filling them up with the golden liquid. Errol had come forward, his anger and concern over-ridden by his desire for alcohol.

"Ah, big fella," the Irishman smiled. "See, the power of grog. We're all friends again."

Errol said nothing, reaching through to take his glass. They all swigged the contents in quick succession.

"Right, just the one more and then we'll put her away. Still got work to do."

Stan refilled the glasses.

"Nice rig."

"She's my beauty."

Stan took the bottle and put it back downstairs. He opened the door on the far side of the room. It lead to a bedroom, a spotlessly made bed filling most of the space. He quickly looked through the cupboards at the side of the bed.

And there it was. A thirty-eight revolver. He clicked out the cylinder to confirm it was loaded, and satisfied, stuffed the gun into his belt at the back of his pants and walked back outside.

"We're not far off," said the Irishman. "It's not so far."

Stan stood at his shoulder. He looked at the radar screen and could see something directly ahead of them. He looked up and could make out the silhouette of the island.

"So there's no-one else on this island?" asked Stan.

"No, been here before, quiet as a church graveyard."

The Irishman eased the throttles down and the big boat slowed, settling lower in the water.

"Keep you eyes peeled for feckin rocks. We don't want to be holing me beauty now. Take this and go forward," he said, handing a spotlight to Stan. Stan climbed up on the boat's long nose and walked to the safety rail, pointing the light into the water ahead of them.

"Point it out ahead, and look for the small bay."

Stan did as he was bid.

"Dere she is, hold it dere," said the Irishman. The boat moved slowly forward under low power, into the small bay.

"Now, around to ya right."

Stan swung the light to reveal an old rickety looking jetty.

"That'll be us lads," said the Irishman. "Big fella, drop those fenders over the side, like a good man."

Errol walked along the side of the boat pushing the sausage-like objects over the edge.

The Irishman manoeuvred in close to the jetty, the fenders barely compressing under the slightest of nudges. The Irishman ran forward to secure a rope, and then ran to the stern to do the same.

"Right lads, dats us den. Let's get these feckin things onto your little piece of paradise."

It was much easier unloading than loading had been. The boat was almost level with the boards of the old jetty. They moved the packages quickly across.

The Irishman went below and came back carrying a box and a bag.

"A few things to make your stay a little more comfortable. Dere's not monogrammed robes but dere's everyting you should need. And I've even put in a little surprise for ya. It's the kinda man I am."

He put the packages onto the jetty.

"As I said, the big boat should be along some time tomorra. But if it were me, I'd move these feckin things," he nodded towards the packages, "out of sight and into the bush until the boat comes. You wouldn't want to be explaining yourself to the authorities, now would ya."

He gave a laugh and walked forward to cast off. Stan undid the rear rope and dropped it into the boat.

"Tanks," said the Irishman. Without another word, he fired the big engines, eased away from the jetty, turned around and powered out to sea. Errol and Stan stood watching as the boat disappeared around the island, the engine noise diminishing.

"Let's just leave the fuckin' things here." This was Errol's first contribution.

"Errol, don't be daft. The Irishman's right. What if someone turns up here. You want to explain it?"

"Yeah, and how are we gonna explain ourselves. We swam out here for a break?"

It was a rare moment, thought Stan, but Errol had made a lucid, relevant point.

171

"Yeah, we'll need to come up with a story if anyone sees us. Best if we stay out of sight."

They heaved the packages, one at a time, up off the jetty, carry them into the bush beyond. Once they were on solid ground, Stan could make out an old hut ahead of them in a clearing.

"Let's walk this way." said Stan, who was having to walk backwards. "Behind this cabin and into the bush a bit."

Errol mumbled something uncomplimentary but complied. They moved the other two pieces and then retrieved the packages that the Irishman had left. They carried them back to the clearing in front of the cabin to a big ring of rocks where fires had been lit before. They both sat on a big log. Errol fished through the box.

"Baked beans, champion. And hot dogs, and some stew thing. Not bad," was Errol's considered culinary opinion. "And some tea bags and a pot, I could murder a brew."

From the other bag Stan pulled out two cheap sleeping bags and a roll of toilet paper.

"What about water?" he asked.

"Four big ones," said Errol, "plenty. And this," he added with a big grin. "The fuckin' mad Mick wasn't all bad." He was holding the three-quarter-full bottle of whisky.

"Party night on the island," said Stan. He didn't mention the gun in his belt.

There was already a pile of driftwood near the ring of rocks. It didn't take long to have a fire going and some beans and franks spluttering in the pot. They passed the whisky backwards and forwards between them. Things weren't so bad.

Maria arrived with our coffees and ouzo. Once she had gone, it was Stavros who spoke first, in Greek.

"He says," said Anna, "we can land on the other side of the island without anyone knowing, and walk across, it is only a small island."

"And what do we do when we get there, if they're there?"

"How do you say, that is the thousand dollar question."

I laughed.

"The Greek economy must be in a terrible state. It used to be a million dollar question."

"You are making fun of my poor English."

"Sorry, I shouldn't laugh. Your English is excellent. I can barely say hello in Greek."

Anna smiled at me. I'd barely had time to think about it, but an ouzo and a rest had calmed me. Anna was a stunner. Dark ringlets, flawless olive complexion, very Greek, very beautiful.

"I think we should stop the two men before the big boat comes," she said, and repeated it in Greek for the benefit of Sergios and Stavros.

"If we can capture the two and confirm that the stolen items are there, then I can call the Captain and get his help. He cannot say no, once we have the pieces."

I looked at her as she repeated it in Greek.

Stavros and Sergios nodded. They were on for it.

"And what if they're armed? Do you have a gun?"

"Yes. But I cannot take it with me unless I am in uniform. I must do this out of my uniform, otherwise I will be in big trouble."

"And if they have guns, we could be killed."

The other two men leaned forward, trying to piece together what Anna and I were saying.

"I have shotgun." It was Stavros, the man of the frugal sentence.

We all looked at each other. No-one said anything further on the subject. Stavros took this as his cue to get us organised.

"We leave early, four o'clock. Sergios will watch boat. Three of us walk across island to cabin. Wake them early." He smiled as he said it.

"We should rest and meet tomorrow. I will ask Althaia for rooms for Anna and me. We can stay here."

"She will ask questions," I said. "What will you tell her."

"I will say we are following up on inquiries," he smiled as he said it.

We all laughed.

"Four o'clock at jetty," were Stavros' final words as he departed.

"I will go and organise room," said Sergios. "I will wake you at ten minutes before four o'clock," he said to Anna.

She responded in Greek and Sergios walked off into the dark.

"I cannot sleep yet," said Anna. "How do you say I am too…"

"Wound, you're too wound. Yes, I feel the same. Should we have one more ouzo, to help us sleep?"

She smiled.

"Yes, for medical purpose."

"Medicinal."

"Medicinal purpose."

"Yes," I laughed, "that's what it is."

Maria came over and stood beside me, her hand on my shoulder. She spoke to Anna in Greek.

Anna laughed and responded and Maria walked towards the kitchen area.

"She says that you are now our writer, here on the island. She likes you."

"They are nice people here. It feels like I have been here for a long time."

"Will you write another book?"

"Do you know my books?"

She looked embarrassed. "No, I am sorry."

"Don't be sorry, they're not really that good. But I will write another one. That is why I came here. Unfortunately, I haven't done much work. But I will write another one. It's about the only thing I can do. I don't like the idea of a real job, like being a cop. Too much like hard work."

Maria returned with our ouzo. Anna and I sat in companionable silence sipping at the sweet, clear liquid.

"Now, I am tired."

"Yes, let's go to bed."

She had a look of alarm on her face.

"No, I mean it is time we went to our separate rooms."

She laughed at me. "What do you say, gotcha."

I went in to pay for the drinks. Maria smiled at me.

"So, more holiday romancing."

I shook my head and walked away. Anna and I walked back to the hotel. I left her at reception with Althaia and went to my room.

Errol managed a little jig around the fire, singing loudly, some bawdy ballad about ships. Stan was content to rest against the log and stare up at the star-filled heavens.

I fell asleep as soon as my head touched the pillow. The next thing I knew my watch alarm was waking me. I dressed quickly and walked quietly into the corridor. Sergios was coming out of the room that Eve had been in, Anna came out of another, further along the corridor. We walked quietly down the stairs and along the dark street to the jetty, saying nothing. Stavros was already aboard his boat. The running lights were on and the engine was idling.

"Come, we go."

We all climbed aboard. I went forward and untied the rope. The little boat moved gently forward into a big arc and back past the break-water towards the open sea.

"You take," he said to me. I stepped up to the wheel without question. I could see the same star I had followed previously, just slightly higher in the sky.

Stavros pulled a thermos from a big basket, and four mugs.

"Stavros," I said, "you are a bloody marvel."

He had even made sandwiches.

"Did you go to bed?" I asked.

He smiled at me.

The water was its oil-smooth self as we motored on in the darkness. Stavros took the wheel back from me after a time and eased down on the throttle.

"We go quiet now."

I squinted and thought I could make out the silhouette of something ahead. It didn't take long before the island filled my vision. Stavros slowed even more. He didn't speak, focused on taking the boat into shore.

Finally he broke his silence, speaking to Sergio in Greek. Sergio took the wheel. He rummaged in the small cabin and came out with his gun and a box of cartridges. He put a few cartridges in his pocket and left the box behind. He handed the gun to me and went forward, climbing down the side and into the water, which came up to his thighs. He pushed the boat back slightly.

"Come now."

Anna and I went to the front. I passed the shotgun down to him and climbed into the warm water. Stavros passed the gun back and then beckoned Anna. He wouldn't let her climb into the water, instead, carrying her to the beach. He waved to Sergios, who reversed the small boat off the beach.

"He will wait, just out."

I handed the gun back to Stavros, who took a cartridge from his pocket and loaded the single barrel.

"Is for shooting bird. No kill man…maybe." He squatted and drew in the sand.

"We here," he said pressing his finger into the sand along the bottom side of the dog-turd shaped map he had drawn. "Other men are here maybe. Not so far. We must be quiet." He headed into the trees, Anna and I in his wake.

It was easy walking to begin with, through scraggly grass and widely spaced, stunted trees. It was dark, no hint of a moon. We started climbing slightly and at one point, had to scramble across some boulders, passing the gun between us. Once over, Stavros came close, his finger to his lips.

"Is not far."

We walked downhill. I was trying so hard to avoid stepping on anything that would make a noise, that I walked into a tree branch. We kept moving downwards. The terrain began to flatten. Stavros stopped suddenly and I walked into his back. His shirt smelled of grilled octopus.

He squatted, beckoned and pointed. It took a moment and then I could see the outline of the cabin up ahead. I could also smell wood smoke. I made a sniffing noise. Anna nodded, along with Stavros.

Stavros pulled the hammer of the shotgun back. It sounded very loud. We moved slowly forwards. Stavros stood on a stick and it crackled beneath his boot. I heard a mumble from somewhere in front of us. Stavros moved quickly, leaving me behind. I walked up beside him to where he was pointing the shotgun at a shape on the ground.

When Stan woke it was pitch dark. He was drenched in sweat, needed water and was desperate to pee. After polishing off the whisky with Errol, he had crawled into his sleeping bag and fallen into a death-like sleep.

He peeled himself out of the cloying bag. His lower back felt sore. He reached around and realised why. He had slept on top of the revolver which had somehow remained wedged in the waistband of his jeans.

He staggered a few steps and bent down near the box that contained the stores. He came up with a bottle of water, downing half its contents in one long pull. He dropped the water then felt his way to the edge of the clearing and had a long pee. Looking down he realised he had slept with his shoes on. He zipped up his fly and was about to turn back to the fire circle when he heard a noise in the bush to his left. Was he imagining it, or was somebody whispering. He took a couple of steps forward and squatted in a stand of trees.

He thought his eyes were playing tricks on him in the dark, as he looked at the shapes materialising from the trees. Holy shit, it was at least two people he thought, no three. And one of them was huge. They walked past him to the fire circle where Errol was snoring. He could hear Errol from where he squatted.

Stan pulled the thirty-eight out of his belt, holding it in a clammy fist. He didn't like guns, had never had much use for them, and avoided them when he could. He wasn't sure why he had taken this one from the boat.

The three stood over Errol. One of them yelled.

"Don't move, we've got a gun on you."

It took Errol an eternity to realise what was going on. He rolled onto his side and sat up, poking out of his sleeping bag like a prairie dog from its hole, taking in the scene in front of him. He could see a huge man pointing a long barrel at him. There was another man and a woman as well.

The other man told him to get up.

"Fuck off, what do you want?"

The big man gestured with the gun to get up.

"Where's the other one?"

Errol looked across to his right to Stan's empty sleeping bag.

"Fairies musta took him."

Before anyone could say anything further, Stan's voice came out of the darkness.

"Drop the weapon, or I'll put one between your shoulder blades."

The voice came from my left, I didn't have far to turn.

He was pointing a gun at Stavros. Stavros was spinning around with the shotgun.

"NO STAVROS," I yelled, thinking he wouldn't have understood.

I reached over and grabbed the barrel before Stavros could bring it to bear.

"No, he has a gun pointed at you."

"Drop it," yelled the man.

I held fast to the barrel.

Stavros growled, but released the gun so it hung in my grasp. I let it tumble to the ground.

"Now step back."

The man from the sleeping bag stepped forward and picked up the fallen weapon and trained it on the three of us. He took a step forward, reversed the gun and struck Stavros a mighty blow in the stomach. A whoosh of air escaped Stavros' lips and he bent double but did not fall. The blow would have killed me. Stavros straightened, saying nothing, giving the man a look that frightened me.

"Big fucker," said the man with the shotgun, "who's the boss now?"

"That's enough Errol."

"Fuck you, where did you get the thirty-eight?"

"Never mind that, what are we going to do with this lot? Who are you? You can't be cops, one of you is an Aussie. Who are you?"

"I am with the Greek police," said Anna. "You have stolen antiquities from the people of Greece. You are in serious trouble and now you point a gun at us." She let it hang.

"Fuck you bitch," said Errol. "Who's holding the fucking guns here?"

"Do you think we have come here without people knowing where we are?" Anna continued. "We are searching all the islands. Soon the others will come for us. And then it will go badly for you. If you lay down the weapons, it will be better."

"Listen to this bitch Stan, should I shoot her?"

"Errol, stop being an idiot. Lady, stop speaking, it'll be better for you, I assure you."

Stan didn't know what to think or do. They were trapped on this tiny island with some serious contraband and pointing guns at three people, one of whom was likely to be a cop.

"Sit on the log, all of you," said Stan gesturing with gun. He needed time to think.

I grabbed Stavros by the arm and led him there, worried that he might get himself shot, either because he would do something rash, or not understand what he had to do.

"Where's your boat?" It was the guy called Stan.

"We were dropped off," Anna piped up, before I could speak. "As I said, they will be back for us soon."

The two men looked at each other. The one called Stan gestured to the other to follow him. They moved away but were in full view.

"What do we do?" Errol asked.

"Two things I reckon," Stan had thought quickly. He knew if he didn't have a plan, Errol might start making decisions for himself, and that wouldn't be good.

"They might have a boat on the other side of the island, she might be lying. That's the direction they came from. One of us could go take a look, I don't reckon it's very far. If there's no boat then we keep an eye on them and hope that our ride turns up before theirs. If there is a boat, we can decide what to do then."

"If there is a boat, why don't we waste them. They've seen us, they can identify us."

"Look, let's not be in rush to kill people alright. Why don't you go take a look for the boat. It's getting light, it won't take you long. If there's one there, drive it around here." Stan would have been happy to go himself but was nervous that Errol might do something stupid while he was gone. He was convinced, however, that Errol wouldn't go for it, wanting the easy job, watching the hostages.

"Righto, I'll go," said Errol.

"Really?"

"What. Fuck off. Why?"

"No, no. That's good."

Stan was amazed. He pointed into the trees.

"That's the way they came from, head straight through there," he said gesturing into the bush.

Errol headed off into the growing daylight. He smirked to himself. Dumb shit, he thought. Anything goes wrong and I'm outta here.

Stan walked back and sat on a log on the opposite side of the fire circle, the gun held lazily by his side, while Errol walked off into the bush.

"Let's relax for now and everything will be alright," he said. "Do as we say and no-one gets hurt."

It was obvious that this guy was the more reasonable of the two. I think we would have been in danger if we'd been left alone with the other one. And I think this one knew it.

"You will not get away from here," it was Anna. I think she must have had the same thoughts about this guy. "It is not too late to stop this."

"Lady, it's beyond too late."

"You mean the boy?" I said, I needed to know.

He flinched, I had hit a nerve. In hindsight it probably wasn't the smartest thing to do, baiting the man with the gun, but my need to prove I was right got in the way of common sense.

"Why did you have to push him off the cliff? He was a harmless boy. Did you know he had a disability?"

"Shut the fuck up," the man snapped. "We didn't push anybody." The man went quiet. I was going to say something more but he spoke again, staring down.

"It was terrible. The little bugger ran off through the bush. We couldn't catch him. It wasn't our fault. We didn't even know what happened to him. He ran, and we didn't see him again."

Stan paused. The others watched him. The sun was up, casting an early yellow ray through the trees. It lit up Stan's face. It was ethereal. A single tear ran down his cheek.

"I know about his mother, and his sisters. And the farm. I didn't mean it to happen. I wish I could take it back. I wish it was me."

Stan was staring at the ground, almost forgetting the three sitting opposite. He went quiet.

"It is not too late to do something about it." It was Anna, her voice soft.

"It's too late for Alfio," said Stan.

Anna stood and took a step towards him. No, I thought, don't.

"Just hand me the gun."

"SIT DOWN," his head shot up along with the gun. "Sit the-fuck down."

Anna quickly resumed her seat.

"Fuckin' rocks," said Errol when he reached the barrier that had confronted the others. "Just a short walk," he said in a whiny voice, mocking Stan's words. When he had climbed to the highest point he could see water, but more importantly, the little boat lying a short distance off-shore and the man at the wheel.

Errol climbed down the rocks and the descent to the beach edge. He put the gun behind a tree and then stepped onto the sand. The little boat was about seventy metres off the beach.

Errol whistled. He was proud of his whistling. He could do it loudly without the use of fingers. The man's head lifted. Errol waved him in.

Sergios was in another world when he heard the whistle. It had been several hours now and he was starting to worry about what was going on. He looked towards the beach and saw the man waving to him. It wasn't Terry or Stavros. He didn't know what to do. He started the engine, pulled in the anchor and moved a little closer towards the beach, but not too close. He cut the engine.

He yelled in Greek, "who are you?"

"Hello," the man said, in English.

"Ah, hello," Sergios replied.

"Come in and get me and we can drive around to the harbour. It's all sorted and we have the stuff to take back."

"What do you mean? Where are my friends?" He regretted saying it, as soon as he said it. What if the man didn't know they were on the island.

"No, it's okay, your friends are watching the others."

Sergios was not convinced. Why wouldn't one of his friends come and get him. He didn't like this.

Fuck, thought Errol. This isn't going well. He stepped back and grabbed the shotgun from behind the tree and ran across the beach and into the water.

"Stop, don't fuckin' move."

Sergios panicked when he saw the gun. He pushed the starter, ignoring everything that Stavros had told him about the tricky engine. He flooded it, and then it cranked and would not fire.

Sergios looked up. The man was only a handful of metres away with the gun pointed at him.

The water was up to Errol's chest, but he knew he was close enough to shoot the old idiot.

"Give me a hand or so help me, I'll blow ya fuckin' head off."

He saw the anchor rope, grabbed it and hauled the boat closer, walking back to where the water was only knee deep. Errol looked at the boat. How the fuck am I going to get up there.

"Help me you old prick." He could see the old man was having trouble understanding his colourful language.

"Ladder, where's the fuckin' ladder."

The old man reached down and lifted some steps over the side.

"That's better old man, now get back," he said waving the long barrel at him.

Errol put the gun across the top of the boat edge and then hauled himself up. He smiled at his cleverness, getting control of the boat.

"Now, isn't this good. I've even got a skipper," he said out loud. Now what do I do, he thought, sitting on the edge of the boat staring at the scared old man. I'm still better off on the big trawler, than going somewhere in this little fart of a thing. And that bitch lied. So maybe no-one else is coming. He made a decision.

"Right, let's go. Round to the other side," Errol pointed with gun. "Let's go."

Sergios got the boat started, first attempt. They chugged off around the island.

We all heard the little boat a few seconds before we saw it move around the headland into the bay. Sergios brought it in alongside the jetty and tied it off. The man called Errol, the unstable one, prodded him forwards with barrel of the gun.

"Well lookie," he said, a big grin on his face. "I've got us a boat."

Sergios sat beside us on the log, four ducks in a row. I felt a bit stupid.

Errol, the tall one, beckoned the other one, Stan, away from us. No doubt to plan their next move.

"So what do we do?" I asked quietly, mostly to Anna.

"What can we do? We have to wait and see what they are going to do."

I voiced my biggest concern.

"If that big boat comes, they may not want to leave witnesses."

"I too, have thought of this."

It was an awkward pause.

"So what now? If the bitch was lying about having a boat, I reckon she was probably lying about searching the islands. What if we wait a few hours for the big boat."

Stan kept his surprise at Errol's reckoning to himself.

"Yep, I think the same. We wait a while and see."

"How long do ya reckon? We can jump on the little boat, if we need to, and head back to the island and get a ferry."

"Yeah, I reckon we could do that as well, if we need to."

"But we're gonna have to knock this lot off. They're witnesses."

"Errol, I'm not knockin' anyone off…and neither are you."

Errol turned with a leer.

"Says who?"

"Look Errol. If we got caught now we'd get a few years for all this. If we kill someone we won't be seeing daylight again, except through bars."

"Yer reckon just a few years for takin' a cop prisoner. Yer full of shit. We'd get years for this. But if we top 'em, we're scott free. No one else knows about us, except the boss and the other bitch. And they ain't grassin'."

It was getting dangerous, Stan could feel the rising tension in Errol.

"Let's wait a couple of hours and see what happens."

"Yeah, and if the big boat comes, whadya reckon they're gonna do with them."

Stan said nothing in response, but thought that Errol had a point. What would they do with them. He walked back and sat on the log. He picked up a water bottle and took a swig, and then offered it to the others.

"Fuck that," said Errol, walking up behind him. "Nothing for those bastards."

"Fuck off Errol, it's just water." Stan stood and then handed the bottle to the woman. She said thanks and took a swig, passing it to Terry. They all had a drink.

"Mr fuckin' humanity." Errol shook his head. "Big fella, where's the other cartridges for this?"

Stavros gave the man a stare of pure hate. I wasn't sure if he had understood what Errol had said.

"Where's the fuckin' ammo for this? You gotta have more than one shot."

Stavros continued to stare. Errol took a step forward.

I raised my hand.

"Stop, I'll get them." I reached across to the pocket of Stavros' vest and undid the zip. Stavros slapped my hand away.

"No Stavros, no point." I reached in and pulled out six other cartridges and passed them to Errol.

"There, that's better now."

As he said it he took a step sideways and started to swing a back-hander towards Stavros' face. Stavros' hand shot up in a blur and grabbed it. He squeezed. Errol screamed and buckled.

Stan jumped up, pointing the revolver.

"NO STAVROS," I yelled.

Stavros spat out a single Greek word.

"Let him go or I'll shoot you." Stan pulled the hammer back.

Errol was on his knees screaming in pain, Stavros was still twisting his wrist. Errol still held the shotgun in the other hand but could do nothing to bring the unwieldy weapon to bear on the big man.

I grabbed Stavros' hand and pulled him away. He let go. Errol dropped down, holding his injured arm.

"Big fucker," he yelled. "you've broken it. I'll kill you for this." He stood, pushing the butt of the shotgun into the ground to help him rise. As he did he grabbed the barrel and jabbed the butt straight towards Stavros' face. Stavros blocked the blow with his forearm.

Errol stepped back and raised the barrel, pointing it into Stavros' face.

"NO," yelled Stan.

The boom of the twelve gauge almost swamped the crack of the small revolver. It was mayhem. The noise had stunned my senses. I found it hard to focus. I turned, expecting to see Stavros lying over the back of the log, half his face gone. But he still sat beside me, implacably, rubbing at the arm that had blocked the gun butt.

"You shot me, you fucking cunt." Errol was on his knees, his head almost most touching the ground, screaming. Blood soaked down the sleeve of his shirt. He tried to open the shotgun but couldn't manage it.

Anna reached forward and pulled the gun away from him and threw it behind the log.

I turned to look at Stan. He still had the revolver raised. He looked stunned.

"I couldn't let you do it Errol. It wouldn't be right."

"I'll kill you for this." It was said quietly, between gasps of pain.

"Help him," said Stan, to the group.

It was Sergios who responded first. He tried to help Errol to his feet.

"Fuck off."

Sergios shrugged.

"He does not want help."

"Errol, let him help you. We need to bandage you up."

Sergios tried again. Errol rose unsteadily and was helped to sit on the other log. Sergios pulled off Errol's shirt.

It was bleeding a lot from the small hole, no exit wound. Sergios seemed to know what he was doing. He took out a pocket knife and cut the shirt into strips, wrapping the wound tight. Errol grunted in pain each time Sergios pulled a strip tight. At one point Errol almost fell off the log. Anna ran over to help steady the wounded man.

"He will need doctor soon," said Sergios. "The bullet is still in there and he will lose much blood."

Stan had lowered the gun to his side. He stood looking down on the scene before him.

"So what now?" it was Anna. She was staring at Stan.

"I don't know."

"Let's get on the boat and get the fuck out of here." Errol had lifted his head. His voice was weak.

"And go where? I can't take you on a ferry like this."

"No, it'll be okay. If we go now, we can get the lunchtime ferry from the island. Come on mate. Let's go."

"Stan," I said, "give it up man. It's over. You're one of the good guys."

"Yes," said Anna. "You save us, you care about Alfio. Help to make it right."

It was Stavros who saw the big trawler approaching.

"Look," he said, pointing seaward. The boat was a long way off but clearly visible, a trail of smoke in the sky above.

"Thank christ," said Errol. "We can grab that pile of rocks and fuck off home and get sorted."

I hadn't thought about the stolen artefacts for a while, being a little more focused on gun barrels. Anna must've been having similar thoughts.

"Leave the artefacts. They belong to the Greek people. To Alfio's memory and to his family."

"Don't listen to them Stan. We can get the job done, get our money and be home. Don't listen to them. Shut the fuck up you bitch."

"Errol, I reckon they're right. Let's get a ride on the trawler and get out of here. Leave the stuff behind. We've done enough."

"And you reckon they'll take us without the pieces. Have a think. Why would they help us if there's nothing in it for them. Shit, we'll be lucky if they come in at all when they see the boat."

I looked back towards the trawler. It was much closer now. I could clearly see the big sticky out bits.

"Then let us go and hide," I said looking into Stan's eyes. I could tell he knew what I meant.

"No Stan, we can't, they know too much. And if they get help, they can send coast guard after the trawler."

Stan looked from Errol to the four of us.

"Run, go," he said.

We didn't need telling twice, any of us.

"You fuckin' idiot," was the last thing I heard, as we ran into the bush.

"Come," said Stavros.

He led us back the way the three of us had come but then stopped and turned at a forty-five degree angle. We climbed a short rise, into a nest of boulders and then through a small gap into a clearing of sorts, surrounded by trees and rocks.

"Come," we followed him towards a pile of rocks and vines. He pushed through and disappeared. I followed. It was a cave.

31

The small boat shot ahead of the trawler, pulling into the cove, stopping behind Stavros' boat. In nautical parlance it was called a rib, a solid hull, surrounded by an inflatable collar. It was powered by twin outboards and had a cockpit in the centre. The man standing in the bow carried a military style rifle. Another man stood beside the driver, carrying a similar weapon.

The three jumped onto the jetty. They could see the two men in the clearing. They walked cautiously forward, fanning out once they were off the jetty. The driver had pulled a handgun from his belt.

Stan raised his hands.

"Toss the piece."

Stan thought the voice sounded Australian. He threw the gun away towards the men.

"We're with you," said Errol. He was still sitting on the log. He had tried to rise but felt faint and sat again. "We've got the rocks here. There's some other people here. They're hiding. This fuck-wit let them go. He shot me."

Stan said nothing. The men came forward carefully. They looked practiced.

"Where's the stuff?" the driver asked Stan, ignoring Errol's outburst.

"Behind the shack."

"How many others? Any guns?"

"No guns. Four of them. They've run away. They won't bother you."

The man seemed to analyse what he was being told. One of the others had moved around through the bush.

"Is here boss."

"Right let's get it onto the boat and get out of here. You," he said to Stan, "give 'em a hand. And you," he said, turning towards Errol, "shut up, and stay out of the way if you can't help. Or I might be tempted to finish the job."

"But they've seen us," he pleaded, "we need to find them and kill them."

"Righto you blokes, get it done."

He bent and retrieved Stan's revolver and lobbed it over in Errol's direction.

"Here you go, go find them. But you'd better be quick."

Errol wasn't sure the man was being serious. The man turned away to help with the loading. The other two were already carrying one of the pieces towards the boat. Stan and the leader picked up a second.

Errol rose and picked up the thirty-eight. His head swam when he straightened.

"You still here?" the man said as he walked past carrying one end of the tarpaulin-wrapped package. The first package was already in the boat, lying along one side of the cockpit. Stan and the leader laid theirs up the other side.

"Right, two trips," the leader said. He looked at one of his men and Stan. "Wait here, and ditch that." He nodded towards Stavros' boat.

He cranked the starter and spun the wheel. The light, powerful boat shot out of the bay towards the trawler, which was sitting a kilometre or so off the island.

I sat up on the top of a rock looking down over the sea. Stavros had told me to climb up to see what was happening. The others waited in the cave below. I could speak to them through a fissure in the rock.

"I can see the trawler. And there goes the small boat back out. I can only see two men in it. They must be coming back for another trip."

I watched the small boat pull in beside the trawler. I could see the blue tarps being hauled up and into the big boat. It didn't take long before the smaller boat was shooting across the water and back into the bay below.

"They're back again."

It was only a couple of minutes later that I heard the crack of a gun.

Stan watched as the man climbed aboard the small fishing boat. He ducked down a couple of times and then climbed back onto the jetty. The little boat seemed to be sitting lower and lower in the water.

The man stood next Stan and grinned.

"Plugs."

When Stan looked back, the little boat had disappeared below the surface in a burp of escaping air. He watched as the fast boat came back, roaring into the small cove, stopping beside the jetty. The final package was pulled on board.

The leader said to Stan, "get in." He nodded to one of his off-siders. Nothing was said but the man clearly understood what was required. Stan looked up. Errol hadn't gone far. His wound had taken its toll. He stood clutching a tree near the cabin. Stan watched the man walk towards him.

"NO," Stan yelled, "ERROL!"

Errol turned slowly and saw the man approaching, unshouldering his rifle. Errol tried to raise the revolver. The man snapped the rifle to his shoulder and fired in one smooth motion. Errol's head snapped back and he fell to the ground. The man walked over to survey his handy work and then ran back to jump into the small boat.

The driver turned to Stan.

"We don't want to be explaining bullet wounds, now do we? Are we going to have a problem with you?"

Stan kept quiet. The leader started the boat and they roared out of the cove towards the trawler.

32

"They've gone," I said, as I watched the small boat speed away.

"What was the shot?" asked Anna.

I counted only four in the small boat. I knew what the shot was.

"I think they killed Errol."

Anna climbed up beside me and we watched as the small boat was winched aboard. In no time the big trawler had turned and was heading away from the island.

We walked back towards the bay. Anna and I were slightly ahead of the others. Errol was lying in the trees. I wished I hadn't looked. I ran over and grabbed one of the sleeping bags and covered him.

We walked down to the jetty. Stavros' little boat was clearly visible down in the crystal waters. I could see small colourful fish exploring their new home.

"Sorry Stavros," I said.

He shrugged.

"We fix."

"So, how do we get home?" Anna asked.

"You like swim, writer?" The big man was smiling at me. "I have signal."

I wasn't sure what he meant. He saw my confusion and spoke to Anna in Greek.

"He has an emergency beacon in his boat."

"Ah, an EPIRB."

"Someone must swim to get it."

I looked down. With the little fishing boat providing perspective I realised that the water was much deeper than I realised. It must have been more than ten metres. And I wasn't much of a swimmer. But before I could even think about it, Anna had started to disrobe.

We all stared at her.

"I am a good swimmer. Are you?" she said looking at me with a smirk.

When I didn't respond she pulled off her boots and socks.

Sergios and Stavros had turned to face the cabin. True Greek gentlemen. I however, was neither Greek, nor a gentleman. Anna spoke to Stavros in Greek and then looked at me after he responded, pulling off her t-shirt and jeans. She smiled at me and turned, diving into the water.

I momentarily forgot the task at hand as I admired her underwater prowess and the shape of her delightful arse disappearing into the depths. I could see her grab the cabin roof and pull herself down further. She disappeared from sight briefly and then I watched her rise in her bubble track. She broke the surface and held a small orange device towards me. I reached down, grabbed the device and pulled her onto the jetty, and then handed her the jeans and t-shirt. I had one last glimpse of the white bra and panties against her flawless olive skin.

"You are a bad man," she said, looking up at me while she tied a shoe lace.

Sergios and Stavros turned when they heard Anna speak to me.

Stavros stepped forward and took the device from me, fiddling with it for a moment. It began to blink red.

"It is done. We wait."

We walked back to the fire ring and made ourselves comfortable on the logs. Within three hours a Greek Navy patrol boat came steaming towards the island.

33

They were a slick outfit. Stan had to admire that. The rib was hauled up and stowed about five seconds after he stepped out of it. By the time he climbed up the side of the trawler there was no sign of any of the blue-tarped packages.

Stan didn't feel overly welcome on board. The Australian guy, the one in charge of the recovery team, pointed him to the mess room and told him to stay put. There were a few other crew sitting around, drinking coffee and playing cards. *Pulp Fiction* was playing in French on a TV screen. The crew couldn't have been less interested in his sudden appearance. People turning up at odd times and in odd places, things being loaded onto their boat, were obviously common occurrences Stan figured.

He helped himself to coffee from a percolator and sat at a bench behind one of the dining tables. The man who had shot Errol came in shortly after with the other, not the Australian. The shooter spoke to the cook in French and then the pair sat at the other end of the table from Stan. Neither of them acknowledged him.

"So, where are we going?"

Neither of the men acted as if they had heard Stan speak.

"I said, where are we going?"

The shooter turned. He stared for a moment, sneered, then turned away. Stan gave up. The Australian came in shortly after, grabbed a coffee and sat between the pair and Stan.

"You've got a bunk." He didn't look at Stan when he spoke. "I'll show you where it is after I eat."

"Where are we going? How long will I be on this thing?"

"We're heading for Brindisi. It's in Italy. The stuff'll go into a load of fish on a truck to London. You're going on the truck. Should be a day and a bit to get to Brindisi."

"Why did you have to kill Errol?" Stan couldn't help himself. Errol was an arsehole but he didn't deserve to die like that. It was all getting to him, particularly as the reason Errol was shot was because of a bullet-wound Stan had inflicted.

The Australian was stirring his coffee. He stopped, stared ahead for a moment, sighed and then turned towards Stan.

"If you need to ask that my friend, you're in the wrong business." He turned his back to Stan and started conversing with the other two in French. The cook came out shortly after with a tray. It smelled really good to Stan. He couldn't remember when he had last eaten.

"Excuse me, can I get some of that?" Stan asked, as the cook placed the bowls in front of the three men. He looked at Stan and then back at the Australian. The Australian said something in French.

"He'll get you some."

The Australian was young. He was average height and build, nothing out of the ordinary, but Stan could sense something about him. The way he carried himself. Confidence, competence but not arrogance. A good man in a crisis, thought Stan.

The cook came back with a bowl and some bread.

"Thanks."

No response. A few other crew came in at various times. They made no attempt to engage with Stan or the other three. Stan figured the three had very different roles, and probably a different master. The Australian pushed his bowl away, looked at Stan and nodded his head sideways in a gesture that said, follow me.

They walked down a long corridor and into a room with no door. There were eight bunks.

"There, that one," he pointed to a top bunk, and then turned to leave.

"What do I do?"

"Enjoy the hospitality. Eat, sleep, watch a movie. Sounds pretty good to me. There's a shower, that first door back on the left. I'll let you know what you need to do when we get to Brindisi. Don't start asking questions. They don't like questions on these rigs. Especially my blokes."

Stan thought the room smelled like you'd expect a room to smell where eight men slept, after working with fish. Clothes hung from lines strung from the ceiling. Several men occupied bunks, some reading, others sleeping.

He threw his bag up and climbed up after it, and lay down. Surprisingly, the bed was made and had clean sheets on it. There was even a towel. It had been a busy couple of days and Stan was tired. But after a short time he realised that with the events of the previous days swimming around in his head sleep would not come easy.

The image of Errol lying on the ground, a neat hole drilled between the eyes, was a clear picture in Stan's mind. He could see the thin trickle of blood running down the side of Errol's nose and across his cheek. And then, when he thought about Errol, he thought about Alfio.

For Errol and me, dying like this was always on the cards he thought. Probably more for Errol, because he was such a rude, arrogant, prick. But Alfio was one of God's angels. The poor little bugger would have lived a simple and happy life with his mum. Never worrying about the shit going on in the rest of the world. He should have lived to be a hundred. A tear ran down Stan's cheek.

Fuck. I haven't cried since I was a kid. He wiped the tear away with the back of his hand.

Stan didn't speak to anyone for the next day-and-a-half. Plenty of time to think, too much maybe. He saw the Australian in the mess room but made no attempt to communicate with him or anyone else. He didn't even bother saying thanks to the cook, just lined up, collected his meal whenever the bell went, and sat in a corner, alone. The rest of the time he slept or thought about Alfio and Errol, his own boy, and what had happened in the islands. He wasn't in a good place.

The Australian approached after dinner on the second day.

"We'll dock in an hour or so. Get your stuff together and stay here in the mess and I'll come for you." He turned and walked out.

Stan got his gear together and waited. He could feel the ship slow, the vibration of the deck different under his feet. Before long he felt the boat bump and sway and then could hear the noise of other engines and men shouting.

The Australian came back and nodded, leading the way to the deck and then down a ramp to the wharf. It was night time, but the wharf was awash with bright light and activity. Trucks roared up and down and cranes moved about like giant insects looking to grab the next prey.

"This one," said the Australian. He was pointing at a white Mercedes Benz rigid body with a freezer unit on the back, *North England Freight* painted in a cursive font along the side.

"Go talk to the driver, he's expecting you." The Australian turned and walked back towards the trawler without another word. The driver was shutting the rear doors on the refrigerated van. He attached a huge padlock.

"Hey, I'm your passenger."

The driver spun around to look at Stan. He held out his hand.

"Sean's the name, good to have some company." Another Irishman.

"I'm Stan. Nice to meet someone who'll speak to me."

Sean laughed.

"Yeah, you won't be gettin' much of a word out of these buggers." He said nodding towards the huge trawler. They walked back to the front of the truck.

"Climb up and we'll get a move on."

Stan walked around to the passenger side and hauled himself up into the cab.

"Put your bag back there on da bunk. You're welcome to have a snooze whenever you feel like it. Good luck to ya. I won't be using it much. Gotta get dis lot straight back to London. They get a might tetchy if I'm late."

"Thanks. I'm all slept-out after a couple of days on the boat, so I should be company for a few hours."

"Nice to hear."

The Irishman started the engine and moving into the traffic flow, along the wharf. They turned out a numbered gate, crossing rail tracks and onto a street.

"Crazy feckin' place this one."

"Seems like a strange place to unload fish bound for England."

"They don't ask too many questions is your answer. But makes it a feckin' long drive for da likes a me."

They were stopped at a security gate. The Irishman had a clipboard with a stack of papers attached which he passed through the window to the guard. It only took a couple of seconds. The clipboard came back and they moved out onto a highway that ran past the port.

"I've gotta top up me tanks with fuel, just up the road," Sean said, shifting up through the gears. "Last chance to stop for a while. You'd better use da bog and grab yourself a bit of tucker, something to drink."

The Irishman drove onto an access road into a huge filling station, pulling up next to a pump. There were trucks everywhere. Stan walked inside and bought himself some water and a few snacks. By the time he climbed back into the cab the Irishman had filled the tanks and paid. He moved the truck over to a parking area.

"I'm gonna take a shite and we'll be on our way. If you're staying I'll not lock up. Can't trust the fuckin' gypos anywhere, especially here. So make sure you stay put."

The Irishman climbed down and walked inside. Stan sat staring through the windshield at the busy highway ahead of him. An endless stream of trucks from the port drove past carrying containers and other loads, no doubt bound for all points of Europe. The cab lit up each time a truck turned into the filling station. To Stan it felt like the accusers light in a torture session. Shined into his eyes. The questions being asked, why did you let it happen, what are you going to do about it, what would your kid think of you?

What was the fuckin' point, he thought. What happens when I get back to London. Nothing changes, except I'm gonna carry this with me for the rest of me days. I need to do something. How am I going to face my boy?

Fuck it.

With that, Stan slid over into the driver's seat. He knew a bit about trucks. There were always a few around the boss' warehouses and he had been sent with drivers on many occasions. Starting it was no trouble, turn the key and push the button. He pushed in the clutch and jammed the gear shift forward for first gear. The crunch made Stan cringe. He looked towards the building thinking the Irishman would be back any time. He tried again, gently, easing the stick forward. It resisted, so he let the clutch out a little bit. It popped neatly into low gear.

Stan looked around again. Still no sign of the Irishman. He eased out the clutch. The truck lurched and stalled.

"Fuck."

He started it again. He already had low gear selected. He let the clutch out even more slowly. It stalled again.

"Fuck."

He looked around and could see the Irishman, paying for something in the cafe. He started the truck again.

"Parking brake," he said out loud. He looked at the various knobs. It was like the flight controls of a plane. Shit everywhere. But then he saw a red knob behind a metal guard. He pushed it in, it whooshed, compressed air escaped somewhere.

He looked around. The Irishman was heading for the door. He eased out the clutch. The truck lurched but didn't stall. He stabbed the accelerator. The truck shot forward with a roar. He shifted into second. The truck picked up a little more speed, the engine labouring, until Stan flicked down the gear splitter dropping the ratio half a gear. The revs picked up.

The Irishman walked outside and glanced up. The expression was one of confusion as he looked towards the space where he'd left his truck. An empty space. And then across to where it was driving out onto the road. He dropped the bag he was carrying and ran. He was skinny and not that old, and could run a bit.

Stan could see him in the mirror and shifted into a higher gear, this time getting the split right. The truck accelerated smoothly. The Irishman got within an arm's length of the truck's rear.

"Fuck," he shouted. Stan could hear it.

Stan felt sorry for him. It would no doubt mean trouble for the Irishman, but Stan knew his need was greater.

34

A police car was waiting at the end of the jetty in the faint glow of the street lamp when the four of us disembarked from the coast guard vessel.

Captain Danellis was leaning against the front of it, arms folded.

"You, you, in," he said it in English, no doubt for my benefit, pointing at me and Anna. He said nothing more, climbing into the driver's seat.

The Captain had given the matter a lot of thought. The coast guard had contacted him as soon as they had the group—including Errol's body—aboard the boat. The patrol boat's commander had given him an abridged version of Anna's tale about smugglers, fishing trawlers and stolen artefacts.

He also told Danellis that the likelihood of catching anyone was almost nil. The vessel had many hours start into the night. The people on the island were only able to provide a vague description of the trawler. And there were hundreds of fishing vessels plying the waters of the Mediterranean at any given time. Short of stopping them all and searching, a result was very unlikely. Danellis had breathed easier when he heard this.

Now, what to do with his disobedient policewoman. He could have her transferred for this, or maybe even have her dismissed from the service. She could be sent to some regional centre on the mainland and put on traffic duty for the rest of her career. He knew enough people to make this happen.

And the meddlesome Australian. What to do with him? Technically, he'd done nothing wrong. Unfortunately there was no law against being nosey. Danellis understood he was an author of some renown and concluded that he would need to be careful about how he treated him. He didn't want this to become a media issue. He wouldn't like to have to start answering questions about why he hadn't supported his junior officer when she was clearly onto something.

No, he knew the Australian was leaving in a week or so. He would put a scare into him and leave it at that.

When I walked outside the police station, Anna was waiting for me.

"Let's get something to eat, I'm hungry," she said.

We walked to the plaka. Everything was closed.

"What is the time?" she asked.

I looked at my watch. It was midnight. We were both in a daze. It had been a long day. And topped off with a bollocking from the police captain I was feeling shell-shocked. Anna looked no better.

"I'll drive you home…but I have no car," she started laughing. "It's still sitting on the side of the road. Come back to my place and I'll make us something to eat."

We walked across the road lined with tourist shops where the bus stopped and where Stavros had dropped me. We continued walking along darkened streets, turning a couple of corners. There was no-one about.

Neither of us spoke until Anna said, "It is here."

We walked up the entrance path to a two-storey apartment building, up the stairs to the top floor. Anna fumbled with her keys in the dark and eventually got the door opened. Her place was small, a single bedroom and a small living area with a kitchen to one side.

"Sit, I'll bring us something. I don't have much."

She came back with some cheese, bread and the ubiquitous bowl of olives, and a bottle of ouzo.

"A feast," I said.

She smiled and sat next to me on the lounge. She poured two small glasses from the bottle and we both sat back with a sigh.

"Yamas," I said.

"Yamas."

"What did he do to you?"

"It could have been much worse. He told me all of the things he could do to me for what I had done. But in the end he said he would keep me here. One more slip and I will be writing traffic tickets for the rest of my life in some small town on the mainland. And you?"

"He yelled at me a bit about minding my own business, and threatening to load me onto a ferry. But in the end he warned me to stop getting involved in things that were police matters. He told me to go and write a book and sit on the beach for the time I have left here."

"That sounds like good advice."

We both laughed. She turned to me.

"What just happened?"

"I don't know. It's all so surreal. I can't take it in. I think I'm so tired I can't think straight. I need to sleep. I need to get home. Can I get a taxi this late?

She smiled.

"I know your, how do you say it, game? You know there is no taxi so late. But one look at my underwear does not mean anything."

"NO. I wasn't thinking that. Honest. I can get a room somewhere."

She laughed.

"You can sleep on my couch."

"Thanks, I'm not sure I could have made it down the stairs again."

She brought me a towel and some sheets. The couch was a fold-out.

"Good night," she said.

"Good night."

The sheets felt sublime. Cool and lemony fresh. The final thought I had before I dropped off was a clear vision of Anna's perfect form in her underwear.

35

Stan was amazed how busy the road was, even though it was the the middle of the night. And he had to drive on the wrong side. The truck was English.

He kept driving, heading the same way as the other loaded trucks. He had no idea where he was. He didn't even know which coast of Italy he was on. He wished he'd asked where he was at least, but then the idea for hijacking the vehicle wasn't something he'd given a lot of thought.

The road bent away from the coast through an area of warehouses and industry. He was nervous driving the big truck and knew he was going too slow. He was thankful it was a dual lane road, other trucks overtaking him at speed, glaring as they passed. He drove through a couple of roundabouts, slowing, he thought, far more than he probably needed to, as other trucks shot past him. He could see a huge illuminated sign ahead, the Strada Statale 613. He could go north or south. For no good reason he swung south, looking for a place to pull over.

There was another filling station access road and he drove onto it. He stopped the truck in the parking area and set the parking brake.

His hands were shaking. He knew the fear he felt was about driving the truck, not having stolen it. He hadn't given that a lot of thought yet.

Stan was a pragmatic person and he gave his energies over to figuring out where he was. He knew the name of the place he had just left was Brindisi. He searched around the cab and found a pocket of maps over his head. There was a useful one covering southern Europe. He figured it wasn't Sean's first trip.

He found Brindisi and realised he was on the coast opposite Greece. He could see the dotted lines leading out of the port towards a place called Patras in Greece. He was where he needed to be.

So, how do you get a truck onto a ferry? Well, I've taken a fuckin' van across to Sweden, it can't be much different. He knew he had Sean's papers on the clip board. Would they be enough to get me there?

Sean's phone was sitting in it's blue-tooth holder on the dash. He Googled truck ferry lines to Greece from Brindisi. The ferry he needed didn't leave until the next afternoon. There was one to a place further north in Greece which left in a couple of hours, but it would mean a five-hundred kilometre drive rather than a two-hundred kilometre drive from Patras.

Stan didn't like the thought of spending the day waiting for the ferry, people looking for him. He would feel safer in another country. He called the ferry company to see if he could make it in time. It was much easier than he anticipated. In among Sean's clipboard paraphernalia was a company credit card. Stan paid the two-hundred-and-sixty-five euros over the phone. His only concern was that he needed to drive back in the direction he had come and risk being seen by Sean.

And then the mobile phone rang. He pushed the hands-free button but didn't say anything.

"Hello? You there? Stan? What're ya doing in me truck? Stan, talk to me. Do you know what you've done and who'll be chasing you?"

"Sorry Sean, I have to do this." Stan pushed the button to end the call. It rang again straight away but he didn't answer. He started the truck and turned around, heading back to the port. He was already more confident at the wheel.

Sean made the call he dreaded. He spoke to the boss, who left him in no doubt that things didn't look that bright for his future prospects. He was told to wait where he was.

The Australian had just crawled into his bunk. He was thankful the load was gone and he could have a rest for a couple of days as the huge trawler headed towards Marseille, his home base. The legal part of the catch would be unloaded there, minus the small amount it took to fill the truck.

It would be a profitable outing with two jobs on the one boat. He looked forward to spending some of it. Getting on the TGV to Paris and enjoying some down-time with his girlfriend. He was thinking about her and smiling in the darkness when his phone rang.

"You're joking. That spineless shit took the truck? I don't believe it."

He finished his call with the boss and leaped out of bed. There'll be no fucking Moulin Rouge for me just yet.

He woke his boys and spoke to the captain. The trawler was already into the shipping lanes and steaming south from Brindisi. The trawler stopped and they loaded their small amount of gear into the rib and headed back towards the port, the Australian at the wheel.

He landed them in the marina where the yachts and pleasure cruisers were moored. The Australian didn't want to be bothered with port procedures, especially when the three of them were all carrying Glock 17s.

A crewman from the trawler had come along with them and would take the rib back. The three men stepped onto the jetty. It was nearly two in the morning. They climbed into a taxi and went to the nearest hotel.

The Australian wasn't stressed or even surprised about what had happened. A little annoyed perhaps, but that was the business he was in. And he had learned over the years to take things as they came. There was always a surprise around the corner.

His name was Rupert, but very few people knew this, and if they did, were smart enough not to say it. He went by his middle name, Anthony—when he used his own name. He had served in the elite commando regiment of the Australian army, and spent more than a little time in the valleys of Oruzgan Province in Afghanistan.

But like many of his former colleagues, he realised there was a more lucrative market for his skills outside of the armed forces. For the last few years he had freelanced, doing a bit of work for his London contact but always under the proviso that he could come and go as he pleased, undertaking other contracts. Mostly it was security and protection, reactive stuff. But occasionally it was more proactive. Like this job was now.

The two men with him, Leo and Louis, were both former French Foreign Legion soldiers. He used their services from time to time when he needed assistance. They met in his room and he explained what had happened. Like Anthony, neither registered much of a reaction. Anthony called the boss in London.

Stan passed within a few hundred metres of the hotel where Anthony and his off-siders were sitting, on his way back to the port. He had programmed the destination into Sean's Sat-Nav and was finding the drive back to the port relatively stress free. But while the drive was going well, he did have concerns about whether he had the necessary permits and permissions to get his truck onto the ferry. He figured if it all came unstuck he would turn around and hand the truck into the local police.

He needn't have worried. The security protocols, especially for the three-am ferry, were lax. He was waived straight through by the security guard at the gate to the port facility. He pulled into a line of trucks which had already begun moving forward to load onto the boat. It was only a few minutes before he was waived forward. He had his clipboard ready to show but the only thing the crew member wanted to see was his ticket, which was on Sean's mobile. He drove down the boarding ramp and pulled in behind another truck.

His fare included a cabin. The journey was less than eight hours, meaning he would arrive about lunch time. He grabbed his bag and took the phone, taking Sean's advice and locking the truck. He headed up the nearest stairs to the truck-driver's area which was separated from the rest of the passengers. Not that there were many other passengers or trucks for that matter.

His cabin was tiny but functional. He had a long, hot shower and put on some clean clothes. He fell asleep before he had a chance to think about what lay ahead.

"He's nearby you."

"What do you mean?" asked Anthony.

"I mean he's in the fuckin' port area somewhere. I finally found the moron who looks after our tracking devices and he says that the truck is still in the port area."

"How long ago was this?"

"About an hour."

"He could be miles away."

"No, we're getting a reading from that area. I'm looking at it now."

"Maybe he dumped it."

"Hang on," said the London voice, "he's on the move. Doesn't make sense, it's heading west…he must be on a fuckin' ferry."

"Right, I'll check the schedules. It can't be hard to figure out. I'll need to hire a car to follow."

"Spend what you need, I'll see you right. And Anthony, he doesn't come home."

"Yeah, gotcha. What about the artefacts, if it's a problem."

"Nah, I don't give a fuck about them. Small change. Just get the product back."

"Right you are. I'll give you a call when I have something to tell you."

The connection was broken. Anthony sat back in his chair. That'll make it a bit easier, he thought. The gear will certainly be easier to conceal and move if we can't use the truck.

He checked the ferry timetables. There was only one out at that time, heading for Igoumenitsa in Greece. Got to be that one, he thought. He checked the timetables again and the airlines. There was another ferry leaving in a couple of hours. There were flights to the area as well, but nothing that would get him there any sooner. And if he went by ferry he'd have the car with him, and hit the ground running.

36

I woke up when I heard Anna in the kitchen.

"Morning."

"Good morning. Would you like coffee?"

"Fantastic, thanks."

I jumped up and pulled on my jeans before she came out of the kitchen. I pulled the sheets off the bed and folded it back into the couch, pulling the coffee table back into position. Anna came out carrying two small cups, placed them on the table, and sat beside me.

"Sleep well?"

"Yes," I said, "like a log."

"Interesting expression."

"So what happens now?" I asked looking into her face.

"What do you mean?" She looked uncomfortable.

"I mean with the robbery."

"Nothing. Putting aside what the Captain has threatened, what can we do? They've gone. The artefacts are gone. There's no way forward."

"I guess you're right. It feels a bit strange after all that's happened that there's not something that we can pursue. What about Alfio's death? Will anyone speak to his mother?"

Anna frowned.

"It is not something I have thought about. But you are right. She has a right to know. If we believe the man, Stan, then we know they did not kill Alfio, but his mother should know what happened. I will speak to the Captain about it."

Anna smiled.

"But you, you had better do as the Captain advises. Write your book and enjoy the beach."

"And can I see you again?" I had to ask, it was now or never.

She blushed.

"Yes. And now I have to get ready for work. No doubt I will be sitting at a desk for the next six months doing work with paper. But, at least I am still here. You do not need to leave, but there is a bus that leaves soon to your village if you want to get back."

"Yes. I'd best go home and change my clothes. I'll no doubt have a lot of explaining to do to Althaia, Maria and others."

"Yes. I will call Sergios and explain what has happened. Perhaps you can talk to Stavros. Oh, and his boat. I forgot, what will he do?"

"Yes, I'll talk to Stavros. He's a resourceful man. Hopefully we can do something. You'll need to get your car as well."

"I will contact the garage."

Anna went off to ready herself for work and came out in her uniform.

"I must go now."

I reached out a hand. She took mine and hesitated. I leaned forward and kissed her on the cheek. She gave me a hug. It was warm and comfortable, her hair smelled of apples. She pulled back and smiled and then walked out through the door. I drank the last remnants of coffee from the stove-top pot and headed off to the plaka and the bus. I was the only passenger this early. I saw Anna's car on the side of the road and smiled.

I stopped at Maria's for breakfast on my way back from the bus stop. She ran over to sit with me, patting my hand.

"What have you crazy people been doing? Stavros has already been here this morning and told me what has happened. I get you some breakfast and then you tell me. I will call Althaia as well."

I was fairly sure she had called more people than Althaia. Before long there were half a dozen villagers sitting around the table, including Althaia, to hear the story. Althaia gave me a big hug when she arrived. She explained that she had spoken to Sergios already.

I ran through the story in detail, and included the details about Alfio. It was time I stopped keeping it to myself. It took a long time. There was a lot of translation to Greek and questions translated to English. No-one seemed to judge me for not telling people sooner than I had. In fact I was treated like a hero.

"You are a brave man for trying to stop these people and save the stolen things," Maria concluded. When it was translated I received a round of applause. I blushed. Maria shooed them all away, except Althaia, so I could eat my breakfast.

"Where is Stavros?" I asked. Before Maria could answer he ducked his head under the awning and walked to my table.

"Writer," he said, reaching his big hand to me.

Maria brought him coffee and Althaia went back to the hotel to deal with morning departures and check-ins.

"Your boat," I said. "I am very sorry. What can we do?"

He shrugged.

"We fix. Soon, my friend comes with his boat. You come?"

"Sure, if I can help."

He smiled.

"You watch."

I went back to get a hat and some water and met Stavros on the jetty where he was standing near a boat, much larger than his dory, with all sorts of pumps and hosing, and a deck crane. He introduced me to his friend Georgios and we chugged out of the harbour.

It felt strange going back to the island. When we moored beside the jetty the first thing I did was look towards the place where Errol had been shot. I'd seen his body removed by the coast guard crew but somehow I half-expected to see it lying there.

There was a dingy already there when we arrived. A young man, he looked to be in his twenties, was sitting on the jetty in a wet suit. It was peeled off to the waist, showing a well-developed six pack. He worked for Georgios.

Stavros, Georgios and the young man were all business. I stayed out of the way, wandering over to the fire stones. Apart from a plastic water bottle there was no evidence that we'd even been there. I didn't walk to the spot where Errol's body had been.

The young man was already down at Stavros' sunken boat when I walked back to the jetty. He was using a compressor to breath, the long hose snaking its way to the boat. He surfaced and spoke in Greek. Georgios handed him a harness of sorts which he swam down and worked underneath the bottom of the boat, joining up the separate cables above the deck of the boat into one big ring. I could see it clearly through the pristine water. Georgios lowered a basket using the deck crane. It was full of white plastic. I watched as the diver pulled pieces from the basket, disappearing inside the hull with each one.

It was a long task. Georgios retrieved the basket, removed it from the cable and then sent the cable back down. The diver attached the cable to the harness ring and Georgios took up the slack but pulled no further.

Georgios then sent down a thick white hose which was attached to the same compressor providing the air to his diver. He disappeared inside the hull for more than an hour, inflating the white bags inside. Like a giant belch, a huge surge of air bubbles would come out of the little boat from time to time.

The diver eventually showed himself, looked up and gave the thumbs up. He hung on the cable and watched the boat beneath. Stavros sat on the edge of the salvage boat saying nothing, looking down into the depths.

It was like a battle between the various elements of the process: cable, bubbles, steel arm, engine and even the diver. The revs on the engine increased, the crane's arm creaked, the boat was forced lower into the water. The revs increased slightly. I held my breath. But then I realised that the little boat was slowly rising off the bottom. The diver had risen and was near the surface now, and showed his hand, in a 'stop' gesture. Georgios held Stavros' boat where it was and the diver swam down.

He swam all around the outside of the hull and then onto the deck to look inside. Satisfied that all was well, he gave Geogios another thumbs-up. The little boat rose quickly. The diver had to move out of the way as the deck cleared the surface. Georgios passed another hose to the diver who plunged it down inside the hull. Georgios started another engine and water began pouring out another hose over the side of the salvage boat.

Stavros looked around and smiled, firstly at Georgios and then at me. He helped the young diver back onto the salvage boat and patted him on the back. The big fisherman stepped onto the jetty and stood next to me.

"Is good, very good."

I walked back to the cabin and the fire ring, sitting for a moment on the log where I had sat only a couple of nights before with a gun pointed at me.

It took more than an hour to pump the water out of Stavros' boat. The gear was packed and a tow-rope attached for the slow journey back to the port with Stavros steering his little boat. By the time we came around the break-water the sun was setting.

Stavros looked very happy. From what I could see the boat looked to be in good fettle. Stavros explained that he would check the engine tomorrow, pull it apart and clean it thoroughly. But he did not anticipate any problems. It was a strong engine, he said.

While Stavros was busy on his boat, I asked Georgios how much he would charge Stavros. His English was poor and he looked to the young diver, who had followed us back to port. He explained what I was asking, in Greek. I said that I wanted to pay the fee.

Geogios smiled, understanding. It was four hundred euros. I asked him to wait and went back to my room. Four hundred represented the lion's share of my holiday funds, but I didn't care. This was important to me. I walked back to the jetty and handed the money to Georgios and shook his hand. He climbed into his boat, chugged out of the harbour, heading for his village along the coast.

Stavros had his head stuck inside the cabin of his boat.

"Stavros, maybe an ouzo and coffee?"

The big head came about, all accordion keys on display.

"Yes, is good."

We walked back towards Maria's place. He put an arm around my shoulder.

"My friend."

37

Stan woke in a panic, arms flailing, pulse racing.

He had no idea what had woken him, but wasn't surprised given the present circumstances. He checked Sean's phone. It was almost eleven in the morning. At least he'd had a decent sleep. Now for some food. He dressed and stepped outside into the corridor. The driver's dining room was close by. Like the cabin, the meals were free for truck drivers. There were a handful of other drivers sitting around, drinking coffee, reading papers or talking together.

He got a nod from a couple. He laughed as he turned towards the carvery. If they only knew.

Breakfast was good. Eggs, bacon and hash browns—shame they didn't have beans—and a big mug of coffee. He found a quiet spot with a window looking out over the calm sea. There was nothing to see, no land in the distance, no other ships.

He'd brought the map from the truck and sat it on the table. He unfolded it and then refolded it, leaving the area of Greece that he needed on a single panel. Google said it was nearly five hundred kilometres to Athens. It would take the best part of a day, the roads looked windy and hilly. Looks like a night in the truck somewhere before Athens, he thought.

The ferry that he needed, the same one that Errol and he had used to take the van to the island, left at eight o'clock in the morning. That would work well.

He used the phone to book and pay for a passage for the truck. It was going well.

He had a second coffee, went back to the cabin and had another shower. By the time he had packed his gear it was time to head down to the truck. As he walked he felt a mixture of anxiety and excitement.

It was the right decision. He knew that now. It wasn't enough to get out of the business and set himself straight. He needed to do something, draw a line somewhere. Something that might go some way to atone for the things he had done over the years. But it was the things he had done recently that he wanted to make right. It was the stolen artefacts, it was Errol's death. But most of all it was Alfio. That's what's driving me, he thought. I can't bring him back but I can pull something good from this awful load of shit.

He unlocked the truck and climbed into the cab. He was actually feeling a bit excited about the drive. His confidence behind the wheel had grown and it was a nice machine to drive. The green light came on in the ferry bay and he turned the key and pushed the button to start the big engine. It kicked into life and idled smoothly. The doors opened ahead of him, clanking down onto the wharf.

He eased the truck into low gear and let out the clutch as the truck ahead of him moved off. His clipboard sat beside him, but there were no port processes. He pulled out through the harbour gates, straight onto the highway, heading out across a flood plain, surrounded by steep hills on either side.

As he looked around Stan had a sense of wonder and freedom that he had not felt in a long time.

Anthony and his boys landed less than two hours later. The trip had been quick. He had hired a car from Brindisi port and managed a couple of hours sleep on the boat. Sleep, grab it while you can, the message drummed into him throughout his army career.

He called the boss when they drove off the ferry. The boss confirmed that the truck was heading along the E90. He said the fool had answered his phone.

"I put a scare into him. Told him that you would be onto him before much longer and that he should give it up. Idiot hung up."

"You told him that we were on to him? You know what you've done, don't you? You've tipped him off that he's carrying some sort of tracking device."

The boss went quiet on the other end.

"Don't worry, he's not that smart."

"Let's hope not. Give me a call if he turns off the road."

The call hadn't scared Stan as much as he thought it would. He knew the boss would ring eventually, and Stan had decided to take the call. The boss had gone through the list of threats that Stan knew he would. He had railed about ungrateful staff, favours done, moving to the threats. Stan sat and listened, and when the boss finally finished ranting, said "thanks boss", and hung up.

It was part of his cleansing, another step towards his redemption.

And it got him thinking. How did they know where he was? It might have been a bluff, but then Stan thought about the phone. And the light came on. The truck. Of course it would have a device. Carrying illegal shit all the time they'd want to know where it was. Make sure that none of the drivers took off with stuff.

Stan checked the ferry timetables as he drove. If they were on the same ferry they would have me. So when's the next one? Two hours head-start is what I've got, he figured. Two hours to do something. He kept driving, checking the map.

"He stopped for a bit, and now he's on the E90, heading north," said the boss.

Anthony was driving fast, catching the slow vehicle quickly. He looked at the map. Must be only twenty of thirty kilometres behind.

"He must be heading for Albania or Macedonia," said Anthony. "Be a good place to sell the truck and the goods if you knew how."

"Or maybe those sly bastards have set it up."

The boss called again a few minutes later.

"He's gone left onto the E65, heading north. Can you see it on your map?"

"Yep, got you. Looking at it. It must be Albania. I'm only about twenty kilometres behind him. I'll get him well before Albania. I'll call when I've got him."

Anthony pushed his foot down further.

"Alright boys, locked and loaded. We might need to shoot tyres if he doesn't cooperate."

A few minutes more, he thought. And then his mobile rang again.

"Boss, not there yet. Stay calm."

"No, it's the signal, it's gone."

Anthony slowed the car.

"I'll keep looking."

Twenty minutes later and Anthony knew they had lost him.

"Boss, no good. I should have seen him by now."

"Keep looking."

"Roger that."

The young guy who owned the workshop was a marvel. Stan had explained that he thought some bandits were after his truck and his load, and probably had a fix on his tracking device. The young mechanic had pulled the locator out of the truck electricals in only a few minutes. Stan had asked if there was any way to keep it going and take it for a drive up the road a piece.

"No problem," the young guy had said. "I'll fix it."

They looked at Stan's map.

"Don't take it too far, maybe here," said Stan, pointing at a northern road off the main freeway. "You don't want them catching you with it. Maybe twenty or thirty kilometres."

"No problem."

Stan gave him his last Euros and headed south on the E92 towards Athens, as the young man was climbing onto his motorcycle to head north.

There's no truck out here, Anthony thought, driving along the valley bottom. Why would he go this way to Albania? He could've gone up the coast where he got off the ferry, much shorter. He called the boss.

"You say he stopped for a bit. Where was it?"

Anthony headed back to where the highways changed. It was tiny town. He saw the garage.

"Wait here for a bit," Anthony said pulling up out front.

He walked inside, where a young girl was sitting at the cash register. He went back out and into the workshop next door. A young man was working on a car, had it up on a hoist, oil was pouring from the sump into a container.

"Hello, you speak English?"

"A little."

"Just wondering if you've seen a freezer truck come through."

"There are many trucks on this road."

"White Mercedes freezer van, *North England Freight* written on the side."

"No, I do not remember this one."

Anthony looked into the man's eyes. The young man stared back. Anthony turned and walked back to the car. He tried the truck's number.

Stan's phone rang again. It wasn't the boss. And even if it had been, he'd decided not to answer any more calls.

38

Well, I was out of excuses. It was time to write.

It was bizarre, it felt like it'd been one incident after another since my arrival. Like I had an events schedule set out for me. A bit like those book tours I'd been on. Breakfast radio, eight-fifteen, book-signing at a mall somewhere, ten-thirty, boozy lunch etc etc. This wasn't quite as organised but it had certainly filled the time. And then there was Anna.

Stavros had told me to take his phone. Wouldn't hear of taking it back until I was ready to leave. Said he never used it. Although I protested, I was glad. Anna could call me. And she did.

"What are you doing?"

"Some writing. How are you feeling?"

"It feels strange. What is the word, closing? I do not have closing."

"Closure. You don't have closure."

"Yes, closure. Loose ends, you also say. There are still many. I must be careful with the Captain, but I did mention the dead man and ask whether there was to be an investigation. He said he had spoken to Athens and that they were trying to identify him. There is no sign of the trawler. So the artefacts are lost."

"I was thinking that I would come to the village and have some dinner with you."

"I'll check my schedule."

"If you are too busy?"

"I'm joking with you."

"You are not very funny." But I could hear the smile. "I have my car already, was not such a big problem. I will see you at Maria's at seven, is okay?"

"Yes, is perfect."

Well, so much for my writing. It was only an hour away. A swim would be more productive. I ran into Stavros at the bottom of the stairs. He looked very serious, almost concerned. He said nothing, but reached into his pocket and pulled out a wad of cash.

"You pay Georgios. Is no good."

"I wanted to pay Georgios. I do not want your money. It made me feel a bit better about your boat. Please, I want to pay."

Stavros was concerned. Althaia stepped out and spoke in Greek to Stavros. He was obviously telling her about what had happened with boat, nodding towards me every now and again. Althaia smiled and gave me a hug.

"You are a good man."

"Tell him in Greek, that he is my friend. And this is what friends do in my country."

Althaia translated. Stavros shook his head and then clasped his big hands in front.

"I thank you. So come, I buy ouzo and coffee."

"Much better." I could swim any time. "Let's go. Anna is coming."

"Ah, so," smiled Althaia. "Finally, the holiday romancing. She is lovely girl."

For once I had no comeback.

39

Stan spent a happy day driving the big truck. He felt free and could see what truck drivers saw in their occupation. He stopped to go to the toilet and buy some food and water in one of the small towns along the way. He used his own credit card to get some cash from an ATM.

It was mid afternoon before he saw the coast again, this time it was the eastern side of the country. He was on a big freeway now, on the final run towards Athens. He had monitored his fuel and still had more than enough for his purposes. He started to check his map for somewhere to park for the night, close to Athens. He figured to wake very early and drive into the heaving city when the traffic was at its lightest, to find his way to Piraeus.

He pulled off onto a slip road about thirty kilometres short of Athens. He found a quiet road with a wide gravel verge to park the truck. He was dog-tired. He hadn't realised how much concentration it had required to steer the big rig for a whole day. He climbed down, had a walk around, went to the toilet and had a drink. His anxiety had increased as he moved closer to Athens and the island. Eating was out of the question. But it wasn't difficult to fall asleep.

His alarm woke him at three the next morning. He washed his face and walked about for a while to wake himself before he set off in the truck. The freeway was busy even at this time. It was one thing to drive a long distance on country roads, but now he was surrounded by cars and trucks, slowing down and speeding up. It frightened him. The signs to Piraeus began to appear not long after he got back onto the freeway. And it didn't take long before the water appeared in front of him. He had programmed the Sat-Nav for this part of the drive and it was making things easier. With a big sigh he pulled up at gate eighteen. It was the same place that he and Errol had stopped. He felt a lot better now. He could see the ferry moored nearby.

The gate was locked and there was no-one about, but Stan didn't care. He was quite happy to wait. He would be on the island in a few hours. And what was he going to do when he got there?

Anthony and his men stayed in a seedy motel on the freeway. The boss had kept them driving around all evening until Anthony had said 'enough', that they were going to have some dinner and a sleep.

His mobile woke him at two in the morning.

"The fuckin' credit card." It was the boss.

Anthony was used to having to wake and go straight into action but this snippet of information was even too small for him to act on.

"You there?"

"Yes boss."

"He used the fuckin' company card. Know where he's going? You won't fuckin' believe this. The idiot is going back to the island where those stupid fuckin' rocks came from. It could be a trick, but we got nothin' else to go on. Go and check it."

"What time's the ferry?"

"Half eight."

Anthony had switched on the lamp and was looking at the map.

"We won't make that one. Too far. But there'll no doubt be others. We'll get going."

He dressed and woke the others. They were on the road in six minutes, heading south.

Stan wondered about security here. He had his papers but wondered whether they'd be enough to get him on an island ferry. He needn't have worried. The guard checked his ticket on his mobile and waived him towards the ferry where he drove down the ramp and into the gaping maw of the huge vessel. He laughed. He was an old hand at this now. He walked upstairs to get some breakfast, but more importantly, coffee, and to think about what he would do when he got to the island.

Anthony worked his phone while one of his men drove. There were no flights to the island and the next ferry didn't carry vehicles. They would have to hire another one on the island.

They'd get there a few hours after the truck but in a place that size Anthony was confident they'd be able to track the man and the truck. What troubled Anthony was what the crazy fool was up to. He couldn't figure it out. The only conclusion he could come to was that he was taking the artefacts back.

He called the boss to explain what was happening.

"Does this idiot even know what's in the truck besides the rocks?"

The boss paused.

"You know, I doubt he does. Fuck, I would've given him the rocks for the other stuff…no I wouldn't."

"Well, he's in for a bit of a surprise, if he gets a chance to unpack it."

"Yeah, that's where you come in, and why I pay you so much, to make sure he doesn't unpack it."

"I'll do what I can. As always, it's fluid, no guarantees."

"I've got a contact on the island, the local police chief. He's helped me out on a few occasions with a few things." The boss was thinking out loud. "But I might leave him out of this for now. He doesn't approve of what's in the truck. And if he's forced to intervene I'm not sure how he'll react. Nah, better if we get this done without him, if we can."

Eve was excited, pacing the gallery a little more impatiently than normal. She expected to hear from her associate any day now. And then she could make herself comfortable and absorb them with her eyes and her touch. She smiled, it was almost sexual.

When Stan steered his rig up the ramp and on to the island's jetty he had a plan of sorts. He drove slowly through the quiet village past the spot where he and Errol had met with the woman. It was all a bit surreal. It seemed a life-time ago. And it felt like his life had taken a huge circle, which technically it had he realised. He felt good. He felt in control for the first time in as long as he could remember. Stan slapped the steering wheel and laughed out loud.

The fish were his biggest concern. He hadn't yet looked in the back of the truck, but he had a fair idea about what he'd find. Boxes and boxes of frozen fish, stacked to the roof. Many tons. The pieces would be buried at the front.

It seemed a terrible waste to him, for the fish to spoil, but he didn't know what else to do with it. He'd thought about selling it. But wasn't confident that anyone on the island would have the facilities to store that much fish, even if he was practically giving it away. And what if I caused a drop in fish prices. That'd be great, I could add fisherman to the list of people I'd messed up. No, that was it, he decided, I'll have to dump it.

He drove up the climb out of the village. He'd need a quiet spot to do it. There were only two places he knew. The rough track down to the bay where they'd met the smuggler boat, or the road to the ruins, where him and Errol had lugged the first two pieces. There'd be no-one using the rough track he thought, but he was frightened he might put the truck over the edge. It had to be the other road. And hope that no-one came driving along.

He drove in about a kilometre and stopped where trees overhung the road and the valley dropped away along one side. He parked the truck as close as he dared and then walked to the back with the keys and opened the lock. A wall of blue confronted him. This was a lot of fish.

It was packed into plastic boxes with lids. The boxes had interlocking ridges on the top and bottom so they could be stacked, without moving. He pulled the first box down from the top of the stack, sat it near the door, climbed down and then emptied it over the bank. He couldn't bring himself to throw the boxes down into the bush. He was done with things like that. He would empty them one by one and leave the boxes stacked beside the road. Someone would find a use for them.

It would take a long time, but he wasn't in a hurry. He smiled as he removed the second one. What did they call it? When those monks would make their backs bleed? This was part of his atonement, his penance.

Anthony and his men stepped off the ferry into the bright afternoon sun. They walked along the jetty and down the street running along the harbour.

"You boys wait there," he said pointing to the taverna, "I'll hire us a car. Order me something to eat."

It took him only a few minutes to organise a vehicle. He asked about a big truck coming through the village. The woman on the desk said she had seen a big van coming through, the kind that would carry fish or meat. Anthony thanked her and headed back to the cafe, stepping aside to let a huge Greek man get to his table.

Anthony sat and pulled out his phone.

"Boss, yeah, just arrived. The truck was here ahead of us, someone saw it. Not here now but I don't imagine it'll be hard to find."

He broke the connection.

"What did you get me?"

"Meatballs and red sauce."

Anthony rubbed his hands together in anticipation.

Stan worked through the afternoon. He was getting tired and reckoned he still had half the load to go. This fish was starting to thaw in the sun. He figured it would start to smell pretty soon. He'd have to move to a new spot when that happened. I'll only take this punishment business so far, he thought, laughing out loud.

I could feel my face break into a grin when I saw Anna walk in to Maria's. She saw me and smiled back. I looked around, Stavros was smiling as well, looking at me. He clapped me on the shoulder.

"Hello," she said in English, sitting down. "Not too much ouzo I hope."

We laughed. Stavros went into a long monologue in Greek. When he was finished, Anna turned to me.

"You are a nice man to do that for Stavros. I should pay some of this too."

"No, no. It's done now, can we please forget about it."

Stavros said something more in Greek and then rose. He clapped me on the shoulder again.

"Writer, I see you later." He turned and walked off.

"My big Greek friend," I said with a laugh.

I asked her how things were with the Captain.

"He is a little distant, is this a good word?"

"Yes, a great word."

"He is distant but I think it will be okay. I think he must punish me a little. But if he didn't like me any more, he would have sent me away."

I looked around to make sure no one was listening.

"Do you think he should have done more to help?"

She didn't speak for a period and when she did, she looked troubled.

"I only say this to you. But yes, he should have done more. All other times I have seen him work with cases, he is efficient, very smart, quick and good decisions. But this. This one makes me worried."

"What do you mean, worried?"

She scrunched her face, not wanting to say the words that were there. She looked around before speaking.

"Worried that he is maybe involved."

"Holy crap." I looked around as well. We were doing our best to tell anyone watching that we were talking about controversial things. "Why?"

"I think about it a lot. He tried to make me drop this several times, especially where this woman is involved. It is just a feeling, and I have no proof, so we must not discuss this with anyone. Please."

"Of course not. I would never do that. Can we do anything more?"

"I am not sure."

The sun was setting and Stan was still not finished. He decided to call it a day. As soon as he climbed into the confines of the cab he realised that he smelled of fish.

He stripped off his clothes and washed his arms as best he could with the little bottled water he could spare, and changed into another t-shirt and jeans, neither clean, and left the fishy clothes outside. He was tempted to drive back into the port village and get some food and more water. Why not, he thought. I can leave the truck on the edge of town. It'll be dark by then.

He turned the rig around and headed back to the main road.

Anthony and his men finished their meal and climbed into the little red four-door sedan. Anthony paused.

"Wait here a sec."

He walked back into the rental shop and came out a few minutes later.

The men looked at him expectantly when he climbed back into the car.

"Just checking where the artefacts were taken from. That's the places we can check first. If he's having an attack of conscience, then that's where he'll be. Putting them back."

They drove up the road away from the port village.

"Take the left up ahead," said Anthony to the man driving.

Stan felt guilty about stinking up the front of his truck. And he felt dirty in his clothes. He needed a shower. He slowed for the intersection with the main road. He turned left, heading for the main town.

The three men drove along the road towards the ruins. It was almost dark and they saw no one. But then they saw the pile of neatly stacked boxes.

"What the fuck? It's the fish boxes."

They climbed and could see the fish scattered down through the rocks.

"Bizarre," said Anthony. "See if there's any sign of the dope."

After a search, Anthony rang the boss to explain the strange scenario.

Stan drove into town and turned along the back street that he and Errol had always used, parking near the house, leaving the windows down a fraction. He walked towards the town centre and into the first of the small hotels he came to and took a room. He asked if it was possible for someone to wash his clothes early. The woman on the desk promised to have them back to him before ten the next morning.

After the woman took his clothes away, Stan had a long hot shower and then lay on the fresh sheets. This was good. He decided not to worry about food tonight, and go for a good breakfast once he had his clothes back. He had booked the room for several days.

Anthony decided to call it a night. They'd also driven to the ruins at the northern coast, where the single piece had been stolen. They didn't see the truck. Anthony had asked some people at the ruins if they knew about the stolen piece and where it had been taken from.

When they pointed to the spot it was obvious that nothing had been returned.

They drove back to the capital where Anthony paid for three rooms.

40

Stan had his clothes by half-nine the next morning. He was ravenous, not having eaten anything since the ferry ride the day before. He sauntered down to the plaka to the place where he and Errol had eaten and where he knew he could get bacon, eggs and beans. It was a stunning morning, he thought. Warm but not yet hot, and clear. He was feeling good.

He'd decided he would get rid of the rest of the fish today and then clean the front of the truck so it didn't smell. He'd thought it through. It was a kind of ritual he'd created in his mind. He'd throw his fishy clothes away after cleaning the cab, and then tomorrow he'd return the pieces. Firstly the one on the northern coast. He'd do that one early, maybe four o'clock in the morning, reducing the risk that anyone would see the truck there—not that it really mattered if someone saw the truck, he was going to dump it.

Then he'd drive as close to the other site as possible, where he and Errol had parked, and leave the others there. It was a shame he couldn't take the two pieces all the way to the site. The idea of the local authorities scratching their heads when they saw the pieces in place, filled him with a kind of glee. But he had to be practical, and there was no way he could get them to the site by himself. So he'd have to make do with leaving them at the car park.

And then he could leave his truck and start fresh. He had no idea where he was going to go or what he was going to do, just that it didn't involve London. He felt clean and light.

And then he saw the Australian.

Anthony had decided he would leave his men at the sites. One at the ruins on the north coast and the other at the end of the road near the port village ruins. They both had phones. He would cruise the island roads. He was still confident that they would find Stan and the truck quickly.

"Come on, let's go," he said. The three headed back to the red car and drove away, to the north.

Stan's heart almost stopped. He stepped back into the doorway of a tourist shop. He had no doubt it was them. He mightn't have noticed the off-siders but he would never forget the Australian. The three of them were sitting at the same cafe where he'd been heading. They didn't stay much longer, rising and walking across the street and climbing into a small red car. He watched as they drove out along the road towards the northern coast.

What do I do?

Stan had lost his appetite. He walked back to his room and studied his map of the island. I've got to dump this fish quick. The appearance of the Australian had killed any happiness he had felt the previous night for the task ahead.

Now it's a matter of getting it done without getting caught, he thought. Caught, or more likely, killed. They're not going to want to drag me back to London for punishment, no, they'll do me here.

Maybe he could park the truck next to the police station and call them to tell them to check inside. The artefacts would go back, he thought. And he could take off, call from Athens. But he knew he wouldn't. He needed to do this.

Anna walked across the plaka, a smile on her face, heading for work. All in all, she thought, things were okay. She still had her job. As annoyed as the Captain was with her, he hadn't sent her away. She figured he'd be angry and short with her for a while, but she knew she could weather it. And now there was Terry. He would leave soon, so she should not get too excited about anything, she thought. But there was something about him.

And then she did a double take. It was Stan walking out of a tourist shop. It couldn't be. She moved closer. He was focused on something. He was watching a red car drive along the road. She stepped into the cover of a nearby shop. It was definitely him.

Her first instinct was to arrest him. But she balked. What would happen if she dragged him back to the police station? Still no evidence. And what would the Captain say, or worse, do to her?

Let's see where he goes, she thought. I wish I wasn't in uniform.

She followed him past the museum and through a couple more turns. This is the same direction where Terry had seen the white van, she thought. The street opened out. She watched as he walked to a big white truck, climb inside and start the engine.

She turned and ran as hard as she could back towards her house. It took her a few minutes. She climbed into her old car and took a punt that he would be heading for the main road to the south, driving there directly rather than heading back to the where the truck had been parked.

She got to the road just as he was driving out of town ahead of her. She breathed a sigh of relief. It gave her a little time to think. She pulled back from the truck. It was large and very easy to see. She'd have no trouble following it discreetly, even in her old bomb.

She called the police station and spoke to the desk officer and explained that she was not well. And that she would maybe be in later. Here I go again, she thought. Next, she called Terry.

I sprinted up the hill and across the plaka, praying that Stavros was home, breathing a sigh of relief when the big head poked around the corner of his house at my knock.

"Writer."

"Quick we must go."

We climbed into the old Citroen and headed out of the village towards the main town.

Stan was keen to get off the main road as quickly as possible, and get rid of the remainder of the fish. He knew they'd be looking for him along this stretch. He figured they'd gone to the northern ruins. That would be logical, he thought, once they realised why he'd come back to the island. And then they'd likely drive along the road towards the other ruins.

He turned onto the side road he'd found on the map. He might have thought differently about it had he known it was the road to Alfio's village. He drove slowly along the valley bottom looking for a likely spot to dump the fish. He doubted he'd have the privacy he'd enjoyed on the other road, but things had changed. He needed to get things done, and quickly.

And there it was. A rough track into a stand of pines near a stream. He was able to get off the road, not a long way, and not out of sight of traffic. But it would have to do.

He opened the doors and started slinging fish.

Anna had seen Stan turn onto the side road. She called and told Terry before her phone had dropped out. She waited at the intersection. It was only a couple of minutes until Stavros' old Citroen chugged into view.

"Come with me," she said.

They climbed in, leaving Stavros' old car on the side of the road, and headed along the valley road.

Stan hadn't realised that he'd done most of the work the previous day. He'd figured that there were still rows and rows of boxes ahead of him. But as it turned out, when he started a new row, he could see the blue-wrapped packages on the floor ahead of him. He pulled at another fish box, flipping back the lid. It didn't have fish in it.

He stopped dead.

"Holy shit," he said out loud, "no wonder they're keen to find me."

He sorted through the boxes that were left, throwing out the last of the fish.

He stood staring at the stack of boxes holding plastic bags of white powder. Was this the answer to his problem or his death warrant? He couldn't work it out.

"What if he has a gun?" I asked.

"He didn't want to kill us last time," said Anna.

"That's not filling me with confidence."

We could see the truck ahead, off the side of the road. The back was pointing away from us at an angle. The doors were open, things being thrown out, crashing into the brambles beside a small creek. We climbed out and crept forward. It looked like fish. Bizarre. The

245

throwing had stopped. There was still no sign of Stan. I put up a hand and we all froze. I could hear someone moving something inside the truck. I dared a peek around the doors. Stan was standing with his back to me staring at the boxes ahead of him.

"Stan, what are you doing?"

Stan jumped and turned in one motion, his eyes large.

"It's you!"

Stavros and Anna stepped up beside me.

"What's going on?" I asked. "Why did you come back?"

He looked at me. It was like he was pleading and sad, all at the same time. He only said one word.

"Alfio."

Anthony left Leo at the village taverna near the ruins, with the ruins clearly visible from his outside table. Louis frowned. Leo got to sit and drink coffee, he'd have to sit under a tree all day with nothing but a bottle of water. Leo flipped him the bird as Louis climbed into the car. Louis responded in kind.

41

When Stan finished his story, they were all quiet, for a long time. Anna then translated an abridged version for Stavros.

"I saw you watching a red car, was it them?"

"Yes, they were heading off to the north I reckon, to see if I'd gone to the site there. He's probably already been down the road towards the other site."

"I must speak to my Captain, and get help."

"Don't do that."

"We must, we are all in danger."

"He's involved."

Anna spun to face to Stan.

"What are you saying?"

"The woman we worked for told me a few days ago, that she had a contact in the police. If it's not you, then I figure it has to be your boss, someone who's known what's going on the whole time."

I looked at Anna. She said nothing, staring at the ground. She turned to face me.

"Your instincts were right," I said.

"I wish they hadn't been."

"What do we do?"

Anna was quiet for a time. Stan broke the silence.

"I reckon they won't care about the artefacts. It'll be the drugs they're after. This has got to be worth millions," he said pointing towards the blue boxes. "I've got an idea."

Stan drove the big rig back down the valley towards the intersection with the main road, swinging right towards the port village. Stavros and I sat up beside him. Anna had tried to talk us out of it. Stan wanted to drop the artefacts back at the sites. His story was compelling, what he had been through, his reasons were honourable. Helping him seemed the right thing to do. Stavros never batted an eyelid. He had climbed up into the truck. No amount of argument from Anna could convince him otherwise.

Just before the intersection, I turned to Stan.

"You know where this road goes, don't you?" I said, gesturing back behind us.

"Up to some little village." Stan was focused on slowing for the turn.

"Alfio's village."

Stan slammed on the brakes near the corner, thankfully we'd only been going slowly. He didn't say anything, just stared back at me.

We'd sent Anna back to the police station. Stan promised that once we had dropped off the last piece at the northern village, he would leave the truck near the police station. The one thing we hadn't discussed is what Stan would do. Could he walk away? Get the ferry to a new life? Did he deserve a fresh start? Being rewarded when a young boy had died? We hadn't talked about these things.

Anna drove back to her flat to leave her car and walk to work. She turned off the main road barely ten seconds ahead of the small red car heading south. She didn't see it.

Stan wheeled the rig onto the road to the ruins. No-one spoke. I was feeling tense. With ten minutes to think about it, maybe it wasn't the smartest thing to do. But here we were. I breathed a sigh of relief when we stopped at the end of the road. There was no-one there.

We jumped out of the truck. Stan opened the rear doors.

"Leave the longest one," he said, as I climbed up, "that's the one for the other site."

We hadn't discussed how we were going to deliver that one. The chances were that we would run into the men in the red car.

I dragged the first package to the rear of the truck. It was awkward and heavy. Stavros grabbed the end and dragged it out, leaving the other end resting on the edge of the truck. Stan grabbed it and they carried it over to the log barrier, laying it gently on the far side.

By the time they came back, I had the second package at the door. I climbed down and walked around the side of the truck to grab the door, to close it. I was out of sight when the red car arrived. I heard the doors open and the men run forward.

"Stan, show me some hands. Stay where you are big fella." The accent was Australian.

I climbed down off the side of the road into the pines and brambles as quietly as I could, sliding over a fallen log, lying down behind it. I could see through a gap at the bottom. One of the men did a lap of the truck. He was carrying a hand-gun.

"No one else," I heard him say.

"Right, up in the back you two." I couldn't see anything. But then I heard a short scuffle and something falling on the floor of the truck.

A short while later the doors closed and the truck started and drove off following the little red car.

I climbed back up to the road, cursing that I had given Stavros' phone back to him. I bolted towards the ruins. I'd never been much of an athlete. And running was for stupid people. But I gave it my best. I was smart enough not to go out too hard. It was about three kilometres to the ruins and then another couple down the hill to the village. I needed to pace myself.

"Boss, yep, got it. Got Stan as well. Just need to dump the truck and hide out for the day. I remember boss, Stan doesn't come home."

Anthony checked the map again, tracing the route along the side road. It wasn't very far which was good. The fewer people who saw this rig the better. He looked in the mirror to make sure it was still close behind.

He turned and looked for a likely spot. When he saw the fish boxes he laughed. He kept driving, starting to climb towards the village. A rough track branched off to the right into an olive grove. They drove in, well out of sight of the road.

Louis opened the rear doors. Stan and Stavros sat quietly near the boxes of powder. Stavros had blood down the side of his face where Anthony had struck him with the butt of his gun. He was amazed the big man had only been stunned. It was a blow that might have killed some men.

They trussed the two men and left them sitting, backs against the remaining blue-wrapped packages, their feet and hands held together with zip ties, hands connected to their feet with more ties. Anthony checked the ties again, giving the big fella a pat on the shoulder. They weren't going anywhere.

Louis hauled the remaining fish boxes to the rear of the truck.

Anthony reversed the little car up and they filled the hatch with the bags of powder, careful not to hole any of them. It filled the rear of the vehicle with no room to spare.

"Turn it around," said Anthony, throwing the keys to his off-sider. He never left keys in the ignition. The man did as he was ordered, pulling the car around onto the road. Anthony shut the truck doors, and climbed back in the car.

Leo raised an eye-brow.

"Should we not do them?"

"We might need a hostage. I can do it later."

When I got to the ruins, my throat was burning and my legs felt rubbery. The sweat was pouring down the inside of my jeans and my crotch was chafing. But I didn't stop. I ran straight past the stone dais, where I'd first been all those nights ago, and headed down the track in the jog-trot that I was struggling to maintain.

I met a couple at the first bend. They looked startled.

"Got a phone that works here?" I yelled, running towards them.

"No, no phone," said the man, raising a hand, like he was defending himself. He had an American accent.

I ran past without stopping, around the bend. I could see them staring, open-mouthed. I made it through the next couple of turns before my ankle twisted sideways on a rock. I went down hard. Blood was coming from the palms of both hands when I got myself to my feet. I sat on a rock at the side of the track, head swimming with dizzyness.

"Get up arsehole!" I yelled, clambering to my feet setting off again. My ankle throbbed. I walked for a dozen strides until the pain eased a bit and then broke into my jog-trot.

Anthony drove to the village on the north coast to collect Leo. The three drove back towards the capital, parking in a quiet back street.

"Get back to your rooms," Anthony said. "We'll spend the day here and head off when it's dark. Get some chow from the grocery, no other outings, capiche?"

The two men nodded. Anthony headed off to the plaka to the tourist information and then to the hardware store, a couple of streets away from where the car was parked. He bought a sheet of cheap blue tarp, the same type the artefacts were wrapped in. He walked back to the car and covered the load in the rear. Stepping back, he admired his handy work. Satisfied, he headed back to a grocery store and bought some water and snacks and headed back to the hotel.

He paid for another night for all three men, and then went to his room to do what most soldiers spent their lives doing. He waited, and he slept.

When I went past the church at the bottom of the hill, I was almost spent. I struggled the final few hundred metres back to the hotel, almost collapsing into the foyer.

Althaia was horrified when she saw me. I raised my hand to stop the torrent of words that were coming. It didn't help when she saw the blood on my palm.

"Your phone, I need your phone."

She held it out to me and I turned and walked down towards the beach.

"Anna, it's me."

Anna told the desk officer she was going on patrol. Thankfully the Captain was visiting one of the smaller stations on the island and she didn't need to explain herself. She climbed into the police car and headed to the port village at high speed.

I passed Althaia her phone and told her I would explain later. I hobbled up the stairs and quickly changed into some less sweaty clothes and then went back towards the edge of town to wait for Anna. It was only a few minutes before she arrived. I fell gratefully into the passenger seat. Anna started the engine and headed out of town.

"Where are you going?"

"They are not here, that is obvious, we may as well drive and talk."

It was a fair point. Anna spoke first, after a time.

"I must speak to the Captain."

"But if he's involved, you could be in danger."

"I will have to force him. I must threaten him. We need help. These men have guns, as you say. They are professionals. We cannot do this alone."

I could find no fault with her argument.

"They will want to smuggle this stuff out tonight. We know where they left from last time. I bet they use the same route," I said.

"It is a good thought."

"I will come with you to talk to the Captain. Maybe if I'm there he will need to play ball."

"Play ball?"

"Cooperate. He might be less likely to do something nasty to you."

"I am not so sure."

The Captain was in his office when we walked into the police station.

"Wait here," Anna said to me.

"No, I should come."

"No, you must wait here. I must do this."

She walked into the office without knocking. I could see the Captain look up in surprise. Anna pushed the door closed behind her.

She came out fifteen minutes later. She called the other three officers together, speaking to them in Greek. They all left the office. She waved me over and I followed her outside. I looked around before I walked out the door. The Captain was still sitting at this desk. He was watching me.

"He has said that I can use the other officers to search for the truck."

"What did you say to make him agree?"

"It was not complicated. I said I had spoken to the Englishman who said that the Captain was involved."

"Did he admit to it?"

"No. He laughed. It frightened me. But he said to take the officers and search for the truck."

"We should check the cove first to make sure they're not there already, or leaving in daylight."

"Yes, is a good idea." She smiled, reached across and squeezed my hand.

The vehicle was an SUV and much more suited to the terrain than Sergios' car had been. It didn't take long to drive down the rough track. We stopped short, as before, walking forwards carefully. Anna had her gun out. There was no sign of the truck or the red car.

It was mid-afternoon as we drove back towards town. Anna spoke to the other police cars on the radio, but no-one had sighted the truck, or a suspicious red car. We were running out of time. I fretted for Stavros. Stan had chosen his path.

We drove up the road to Alfio's village, past where Stan had parked earlier, and not far from where Stavros' old bomb waited patiently on the side of the road. We drove all the way to the village. Anna spoke to a couple of people, but no one had seen the truck or a red car.

Anna's phone rang. She had a long conversation in Greek, she looked at me several times, concern on her face.

"It was the Captain, wanting to know what was going on. He says we cannot use the other officers at the cove, that if we wish to go there, then that is my decision."

The first the Captain knew about the problem coming back to haunt him was when his attractive young police-woman had stormed into his office. After she left, he called London.

The Captain was not happy. He had warned the man that there were to be no drugs on the island. Smuggling people into his country he could abide, even stealing from the sacred sites, but he would not tolerate drugs.

The man in London placated him, explaining that this was an anomaly, that the drugs were never meant to be on his island. And that it would never happen again. The man in London was also able to ease the Captain's concerns about a potential witness to his involvement. This man, the voice in London said, was either dead already, or soon would be.

The Captain warned the man in London of the police-woman and the Australian. The man in London thanked him, suggesting that a substantial bonus was forthcoming.

We sat quiet.

"We should get to the cove ahead of them and wait."

She looked at me.

"You are not police, you do not have a gun."

"I'm not letting you do it by yourself. Let's go, we can get Stavros' shotgun. I can use that." I said this, not really believing I would add any value. I had never fired anything larger than an air rifle.

We drove to Stavros' house. It wasn't locked. I found the gun and what remained of the box of cartridges.

It was heading towards sundown. The red fingers of late afternoon began to play across the village as we drove out of town. We drove the descent again, along the rough track, not knowing whether the men might already be there. We parked well off into the trees, so the car could not be seen from the track, and made our way forwards again, quietly and carefully.

There was no one in the clearing. We moved back, into cover, lying down to wait. We didn't even know if they would bring Stavros and Stan with them. I didn't want to think it, but they could already be dead. Why would they drag them down here? They certainly wouldn't bring the truck down here, would they? But what other option did we have, but to wait and see. And maybe we were in the wrong place? Would they use the same departure point twice? Did professionals do that?

It wasn't long before I had the answer to my last question.

Anthony turned the little car up the village road, turning off to where the big truck was parked. He had warned the men about the police-woman and the Australian. He had expected to see them by now, at least tailing them, if not trying to stop them. Once they got onto the track to the cove he would have lost them, he figured. They wouldn't know the rendezvous point.

"Wait here."

He opened the rear door of the truck a crack, and shone his small torch inside, to see the men sitting where he had left them.

"Almost over boys."

He climbed up inside the truck, pulling out a single-bladed clasp knife. He walked up to Stavros shining the light in his face.

"Your lucky day big fella, you get to play hostage." He cut several ties, leaving his hands bound.

Anthony had to help him to rise, the circulation slow to work its way through the big man's frame. He pressed the gun into his back and forced Stavros to the back of the truck and outside.

"Put him in the car," he yelled.

Louis did as he was ordered.

Anthony pulled the door shut and turned back. The two shots were muffled by the closed container. Anthony climbed down and shut the door, pulled off his shirt to wipe the handle clean.

The car was full to overflowing with humans and drugs. Stavros sat in the back with Leo, who had his Glock pointing into the big man's side.

"Stay sharp boys."

They drove along the main road to the track that the boss had told them about. Still no sign of a tail. Odd, Anthony thought. It was a slow drive down the track. Anthony didn't want to crack the sump on a rock. It would be a long job shifting all those bags from here, he thought.

When the ground flattened out he switched off the lights and sent one of the men forward on foot.

"We'll just wait here big fella," he said pointing his gun casually towards Stavros. Stavros said nothing.

We both saw the headlights at the same time and then they were gone. We probably should have separated to be more effective, but I think we were both too frightened, so we lay behind the log and waited. And that's when it had all gone to shit.

The Irishman was holding the boat offshore and wielding the spot-light while his offsider reloaded the AR15 rifle.

"Easy now, hold your fire."

He was nervous. This was was the most vulnerable time for a smuggler, caught against a foreign shore. He didn't like it. He shone the light over to the left.

"About there," the voice said from the boat. "Put a clip in there."

Anthony didn't fancy loading the boat knowing that there were people out there, maybe armed, and holding the high ground. He'd have to deal with them first. While the guy on the boat sprayed the area he moved around in a classic flank. It was all too easy.

"Righto, hold it," yelled the Australian, stepping into the edge of the beam.

He was right behind us. Where did he come from?

Anna rolled turning her side-arm towards him.

"No Anna," I yelled.

The Australian took careful aim, but then his shots went high, way high. He staggered. There were more shots but they weren't coming from the Australian's gun. The spotlight swivelled back towards the car in the clearing. Someone was standing there pointing a pistol. It was the Captain.

He dived as soon as the light was on him and just before the semi-automatic rifle opened up again from the boat. He crawled forward towards the lip of the clearing, the angle protecting him from the hail of bullets.

There was no sign of the Australian.

"Wait here," hissed Anna, who crouched and ran forward. She

dived flat and crawled forward towards the edge. The light was still seeking the Captain. She rose into a kneel and loosed a clip from her Beretta, the second time she had fired it since the training academy.

When the spotlight moved towards her she dived. The Captain fired.

"I'm gone boys, you want to go, come now." It was the Irishman.

The two on the sand didn't need to be told twice, wading out through the shallow water towards the boat, while the man beside the Irishman poured fire towards the clearing.

The Australian yelled from the sand. He moved forward clutching his side. One of his men ran back to help him through the shallows and then up into the boat. The man on the boat kept shooting, even as they accelerated out into the open ocean.

Anna walked over to stand beside the Captain.

"Thank you," I heard her say in Greek.

A noise from nearby made the Captain turn and lift the gun.

"No," I yelled, "it's Stavros."

The Captain dropped his aim as the big man walked forward. The Captain and Anna walked off to talk. Anna came back a few minutes later and handed me some keys.

"You and Stavros must go. Take my police car and leave it at the edge of your village. Leave the keys in the ignition. Go home. I will see you soon. Please do not say anything that has happened tonight." She spoke to Stavros in Greek. He nodded in agreement.

Stavros and I walked off along the dark track, I still had Stavros' shotgun.

"Writer, you are okay?"

"Not sure Stavros, you?"

"I think I shit."

We both walked into the darkness laughing. Stavros stopped laughing.

"And Stan, he is dead?"

"I don't know Stavros, I don't think it looks good for him."

Anna found us a couple of hours later, sitting at Maria's, drinking ouzo. She smiled at me as she walked towards our table. Stavros rose and gave Anna a hug, spoke briefly in Greek, and turned to me.

"Writer, I sleep, goodnight."

I watched him go, shaking my head. Anna explained that she and the Captain had been nervous about the boat coming back. They had climbed down to the sand and broken every single bag open into the sea.

She laughed.

"I think the fish will be sick for a long time in that area. Stone fish maybe."

We laughed. Then she was serious again.

"The car had many bullet holes. We will leave it for someone to find and report."

"What about the truck? What about Stan?"

"We will keep looking and deal with what comes from it."

"What will you do about the Captain?"

"This I am not sure about. Some things are yet to be said."

42

Anna called me the next morning, Althaia waking me, proffering her mobile.

"A farmer called to say there is a truck in his olive trees. He has not looked inside it."

"Come and get me."

"It may not be so nice," she said.

"Come and get me anyway. I'll meet you on the edge of town."

I leaned across and kissed her on the cheek when I climbed into the car. She almost pulled away, then changed her mind.

"The truck is on the road we have driven, the one where he throws the fish."

The farmer was waiting on the side of the road. He spoke briefly to Anna and then pointed her into the trees. I climbed out, but I let Anna open the truck. She had a torch and in the beam I could see Stan lying on his side in the darkness. Anna climbed and walked forward.

When Anthony had climbed up into the truck after moving Stavros to the car, he walked forward and squatted next to Stan.

"Stan, I'm a bit sick of all the killing and death and you seem like a half-decent bloke. But you have to promise me, that you'll stay out of England for a while and never go back to London."

Stan nodded vigorously.

"I'd not planned to go back, this was my way out."

"Because, if I hear you've gone back, it means my reputation will be tarnished. And if that happens, I'll come and find you."

Stan knew he meant it.

"You've got my word."

Anthony fired two shots into the truck floor, turned and walked away.

"He is alive," she yelled.

I climbed up and ran forward.

"Is he wounded?"

"Just very thirsty." It was Stan.

I found a bottle of water in the front. Stan drained it in one long pull.

"What now?" I asked.

"Too much has happened. The Captain will not want to see Stan." She turned to Stan.

"You may finish your delivery, but then you must go." She looked at her watch. "On the lunch-time ferry."

"I will make sure he does," I said.

She looked at me and then turned and walked back to the car.

"Can we stop here on the way back?" asked Stan.

I knew what he meant.

He got into the cab and fired up the truck, reversed out of the olive grove and we headed back down to the main road.

Sergios was looking out his kitchen window and saw the truck drive down to the ruins. It caught his eye because it was not really a place for trucks. When he saw the men open the rear he became nervous and started walking, almost running, towards the ruins. They couldn't take anything else, surely. In daylight. He was out of breath, wheezing like a pair of old bellows when he summited the car park. He watched as the men removed a package from the rear of the truck.

"Terry?"

"Hey Sergios, present for you."

We carried the package back to the spot from where it was taken, undoing the ropes and pushing it free. It probably hadn't been handled this much since it was carved. It gave me a chill.

"I think if you drive down to the car park at the other ruins, you might find two more packages. Might not be a bad idea to do something with them, before someone decides to steal them."

Sergios stood, his hand to his mouth, tears running down his cheeks.

Stan and I drove back to the village road once more. This time we drove to the end, to the little church on the plateau with the magnificent views. We walked up the hill to the cemetery. Alfio's grave had been completed since the funeral service. It had a simple white marble top, matching headstone, with a white cross on top. The inscription was in Greek. I stood back.

Stan went forward and knelt down. He spoke for some minutes before rising. He was crying.

We walked back to the truck without speaking and drove to the port village, parking the big Mercedes on the edge of town.

"I'll leave these in the ignition." said Stan, jingling the keys.

We walked quickly towards the jetty, the ferry was coming around the break-water. Stan bought a ticket and used the ATM. He handed me a wad of cash.

"Please give this to Alfio's mum, don't tell her why. Just say I heard the story and wanted to do something."

I took the cash.

"So what will you do?"

"I haven't got a bloody clue. But you know what," he said turning towards me, "I'm excited about it. Whatever it is, it will be good and useful. Thanks for your help." He held out his hand. I shook it, and then he turned and walked on to the ferry.

43

The agent and the publisher had wanted the big slap-up lunch in London, but I begged off, thanking them. I knew there'd be a book tour to come and lots of appearances. I could wait. I had things to do.

When I climbed out of the black cab I could see her talking to someone in the foyer. The gallery was elegant, stylish without being gawdy. It was very Eve. I pushed through the door. She hadn't seen me. I waved her staff member away, saying that I would wait to speak to Eve.

I wandered the room admiring some of the paintings. The sculptures were not my thing.

"Terry, is that you?"

I turned. She had that look on her face that I remembered, except now I had a better idea of what it meant. It said *what is he up to?*

"I see you've got a new book out, doing very well I understand."

"Yes, going nicely."

I didn't say anything for a second. I wanted to see how she would react. But, ever the pro, Eve took the pause in her stride, no hint of discomfort.

"So what brings you to London?"

"I was visiting my agent and publisher, they're here in London. But I did want to drop these off for you."

I opened the folder I was carrying. I handed her some blown-up prints. She flicked through. The first three were of the pieces, back in their rightful place. The enhanced security measures obvious. The final photo was a shot of a simple grave in a tiny cemetery, the view behind, infinite. For a moment she let her guard drop. There was vitriol, but in the end I think I saw sadness.

I turned and walked out.

I made the evening ferry back to the island, walking along the jetty, the wheels of my suitcase clacking merrily over the cracked concrete. I could see Stavros' dory tugging on its mooring rope in the light evening breeze, the lights from the tavernas flickering across the harbour's surface.

I made sure that Maria didn't see me. I knew if she did, I wouldn't get to the hotel. But I would no doubt return for dinner.

When I arrived at the *Cycladaen*, the carpenters were finishing for the day.

Althaia was talking to the builder. She saw me and squealed with delight, running up to grab me in a bear hug. She insisted on showing me the progress that had been made, to join the hotel next door to the *Cycladaen*. A lot had changed in the time I had been away. It had been a long month, tying up loose ends in Australia and working through the final touches for the release of the novel. I was happy to be home.

"We will be open in time for the tourist season. I am already taking bookings."

This was my home now. The joint owner of a hotel in the Greek Islands and a writer of some renown. But it wasn't the best bit.

"Hello writer."

I turned to see my Anna standing there.

This was the best bit.

Author's Note

If you enjoyed *Out of the ruins* and have a minute to spare I would really appreciate a short review on the page or site where you bought it.

Thank you.

A big thanks to my great beta readers and supporters Andy, Fi and Clive, for their help on this book and on all the good things to come.

Printed in Australia
AUHW011841220622
365345AU00026B/645

9 780648 421528